ROUND ONE

"Do you know why they call me Grizz?"

"It's a common name for lumps of stupid," Fargo said.

And then there was no more talking.

Grizz waded in, his knobby fists raised in an awkward boxing stance. He flung an overhand that Fargo easily ducked. Quickly, Fargo retaliated with two jolts to the ribs that would have knocked other men onto their toes. All Grizz did was grunt.

Fargo sidestepped a jab and rammed a solid right to Grizz's jaw. Grizz's head barely moved an inch. A huge fist drove at Fargo's face and he got his left up to block it. Even so, the force of the blow rocked him on his bootheels and sent pain flaring down his arm to his toes.

Fargo realized this wasn't going to be a short fight.

THE
TRAILSMAN

#385

THUNDERHEAD
TRAIL

by

Jon Sharpe

A SIGNET BOOK

SIGNET
Published by the Penguin Group
Penguin Group (USA) LLC, 375 Hudson Street,
New York, New York 10014

USA I Canada I UK I Ireland I Australia I New Zealand I India I South Africa I China
penguin.com
A Penguin Random House Company

First published by Signet, an imprint of New American Library,
a division of Penguin Group (USA) LLC

First Printing, November 2013

The first chapter of this book previously appeared in *Diablo Death Cry*, the three hundred eighty-fourth volume in this series.

Copyright © Penguin Group (USA) LLC, 2013

 REGISTERED TRADEMARK—MARCA REGISTRADA

ISBN 978-0-451-24054-5

Printed in the United States of America
10 9 8 7 6 5 4 3 2 1

The Trailsman

Beginnings . . . they bend the tree and they mark the man. Skye Fargo was born when he was eighteen. Terror was his midwife, vengeance his first cry. Killing spawned Skye Fargo, ruthless, cold-blooded murder. Out of the acrid smoke of gunpowder still hanging in the air, he rose, cried out a promise never forgotten.

The Trailsman they began to call him all across the West: searcher, scout, hunter, the man who could see where others only looked, his skills for hire but not his soul, the man who lived each day to the fullest, yet trailed each tomorrow. Skye Fargo, the Trailsman, the seeker who could take the wildness of a land and the wanting of a woman and make them his own.

1861, in what will one day be Montana—where a bounty is being offered for a killer with horns.

1

Skye Fargo wasn't surprised to find a town where there hadn't been one two years ago. New towns sprang up all the time. This one had a single dusty street and barely twenty buildings but one of them was a saloon.

A crudely scrawled sign Fargo had passed not a hundred yards back said the town was called Trap Door. It seemed a strange choice, but when it came to naming towns, people could be downright peculiar. There was a town he'd stumbled on once called Sludge. The name he liked the most was one he heard about from back east. It was called Intercourse.

He figured naming a town Trap Door was someone's notion of a joke.

He didn't know what to think of the naked woman standing in the middle of the street.

Fargo drew rein to study on what he was seeing. Fargo, a big man, broad of shoulder and hard with muscle, wore buckskins and a white hat so dusty it was brown. A Colt was on his hip, and unknown to anyone else, an Arkansas toothpick was strapped to his leg inside his left boot. Women rated him handsome. Men rated him dangerous.

The woman in the street was in her twenties or so. Long brown hair fell past her bare shoulders.

Her head was down and Fargo couldn't see her face. He did see that she was quaking as if with fear. Her arms were across her breasts and she stood with her legs half crossed.

Fargo looked up the main street and then down it and was further surprised to find there wasn't another living soul in sight.

Just the naked woman and no one else.

Fargo gigged the Ovaro and when the stallion was next to her, he drew rein again and leaned on his saddle horn. He was tempted to say "Nice tits" but he decided to be polite and said, "How do you do, ma'am?"

She didn't look up. All she did was go on quaking.

Scanning the street again, Fargo said, "Folks don't wear clothes in these parts?"

Her hair was over her face and when she raised her head just a little, a single green eye peered out at him.

"You shouldn't," she said.

"How's that, ma'am?" Fargo said while admiring the rest of her.

"You shouldn't talk to me," she said, her voice trembling like she was. "It's not safe."

"Safe for who?"

"You, mister. He won't like it. He'll hurt you, or worse. Or his brothers will."

Fargo looked around yet again. Horses were at hitch rails and a cat was licking itself but they were the only signs of life. "Where is everybody?"

"Hiding."

"From who?"

"Mister, please," she said, practically pleading. "Ride on before it's too late."

"I was thinking of wetting my whistle." Fargo hadn't had a drink in a week and a whiskey would go down smooth.

"God, no. You don't want to. Light a shuck before one of them looks out and sees us."

Just then there was a loud crash from the saloon and a burst of gruff laughter.

The woman nearly jumped out of her skin. She quaked harder and balled her hands, her fingernails biting into her palms.

"You have a name?"

"Just go. Please."

Fargo bent down and carefully parted her hair with a finger. She didn't try to stop him. He spread it wide so he could see her face, and a ripple of fury passed through him.

Her left eye was fine but the right eye was swollen half shut. Her right cheek was swollen to twice its size and was turning black and blue, and blood had trickled from the corner of her mouth and dried on her chin. Someone had clouted her, clouted her good.

"Well, now," Fargo said.

"Please," she said again.

2

"How long have you been standing here?"

"I don't rightly know. An hour, I suppose. Ever since they rode in and he got mad at me for not wanting to sit on his lap."

"I need a handle," Fargo said.

"Folks call him Grizz on account of that's what he looks like. Him and his two brothers show up from time to time to have a frolic, as they call it."

"How about your own?"

"It's Candice." She glanced over her shoulder at the saloon. "God, you're taking an awful chance. For the last time, please skedaddle or they're liable to do you harm."

"Where did your clothes get to?"

Candice looked down at herself and closed her good eye and a tear trickled from it. "Grizz ripped them off me after he hit me and I was lying on the floor. He said as how he'd teach me to mind him and told me to come out here and stand until he hollered for me to come back."

"Well, now," Fargo said again. "I reckon I'll have that drink." He raised his reins but she clutched at his leg.

"I'm begging you. Go before it's too late. I don't want you stomped or killed on my account."

"You say he has two brothers with him?"

Candice nodded. "Rance and Kyler. They're almost as snake-mean as Grizz. Rance carries a Sharps everywhere and Kyler is partial to a big knife. You don't want to rile either of them. Both will kill a man as soon as look at him."

"You don't say."

She removed her hand. "Now that you know, fan the breeze."

Fargo clucked to the Ovaro and made for the hitch rail.

"Wait," Candice said. "Where are you going?"

"To do some riling," Fargo said.

2

More laughter and another crash drowned the dull thud of the Ovaro's hooves as Fargo rode up to the hitch rail.

Swinging down, he tied off the reins.

As Fargo stepped to the batwings, he loosened his Colt in its holster. He didn't go in. Not yet.

The saloon was a shambles. Most of the tables and many of the chairs had been overturned. Cards and chips were scattered everywhere. Upended bottles and glasses lay the length of the bar, and behind it the big mirror had been busted.

Along the left wall and the far wall stood twenty or so customers. Almost all were cowering in fright.

The cause of all the destruction and fear were three men. It was easy for Fargo to figure out which was which.

Behind the bar, sorting through bottles on a shelf, was a huge hellion who had to be Grizz. He wore homespun that barely fit his giant frame and sported a bristly beard that hung down to his belt. He picked up a bottle, peered at the label for all of half a minute, and said, "Rum? I had this once. It tastes like sugar water." And with that, he threw the bottle at the mirror.

At the crash, some of the townsfolk cringed.

The two men at the bar cackled.

One had a Sharps cradled in the crook of an elbow and wore a floppy hat. That, Fargo reckoned, would be Rance.

The other was the youngest, with peach fuzz on his chin and an antler-handled knife that had to be a foot and a half long on his right hip. That would be Kyler.

Fargo pushed on the batwings. They didn't creak and the frolickers didn't hear him enter. He took a couple of steps and stopped, his right hand brushing his holster.

Grizz picked up another bottle. "Scotch?" he said. "Ain't they

4

the ones that wear dresses?" He cocked his arm and hurled the bottle at the mirror and more shards of glass rained to the floor.

"You sure are a hoot, brother," Kyler exclaimed. "Break 'em all."

"Like hell," Rance said. "Save some for us to swill."

"Don't worry," Grizz rumbled. "I didn't come to town to get sober. I came to town to get drunk." He snatched yet another bottle and read the label in his slow way. "Rye? Who the hell drinks this stuff." Grinning, he cocked his arm and glanced at his brothers and happened to gaze past them toward the batwings. "What the hell?" he said, and froze.

Rance and Kyler turned.

Fargo let them take his measure. He could tell a lot by their reactions.

Rance's dark eyes narrowed and he began to lower his Sharps but his eyes flicked to Fargo's Colt and he thought better of it. Rance was the smart one.

Kyler put his hand on his big knife and sneered. He wasn't so smart, and would be rash, besides.

As for Grizz, he slowly set the bottle down and came around the end of the bar. He had a revolver and a bowie tucked under his wide leather belt, one on either side of the buckle. "What have we here?"

"I'm looking for someone," Fargo said.

"You're what?" Grizz responded. It wasn't that he was drunk. He was just plain dumb.

"He said he's lookin' for someone," Kyler said, and tittered as if it were funny.

A glimmer of craftiness came into Grizz's dull eyes.

"Whoever you're huntin' ain't here, mister. Go look for him somewhere else."

"Who is it you're after?" Rance asked.

Fargo noticed that the onlookers appeared to be stupefied, except for two. "I'm looking for a miserable son of a bitch. Maybe you know him."

"Oh?" Rance said, and his face had hardened.

"Some bastard who hits women and strips them bare-assed and shoves them out in the street."

There were gasps from some of the men along the walls.

One looked fit to faint.

5

"You don't say," Rance said, even colder than before.

"I just did," Fargo said.

"Stranger," Kyler growled, "you have your nerve. Do you know who we are?" He didn't wait for Fargo to answer. "We're the Hollisters. We do as we please, when we please, and no one tells us different."

"That's right," Grizz said, nodding.

"You'd do best to turn right around and forget about that gal in the street," Rance said.

A townsman cleared his throat. "Listen to him, mister. Get the hell out while you can. They've killed before."

"That's right," Kyler said, grinning. "I have five notches on my knife."

Fargo had heard of some who notched their pistols but never anyone who notched a knife. "That few?" he said.

"Huh?" Kyler said.

Rance had both hands on his Sharps and was poised to use it. "You can't drop all three of us before we drop you."

"I won't have to," Fargo said. "Put all your weapons on the floor."

"Not hardly," Kyler said, and laughed.

"Listen to him," Grizz said, and he laughed, too.

"Is that all you want us to do?" Rance asked sarcastically.

"No," Fargo said.

"What else?"

"I want you to take off your clothes."

3

The Hollister brothers looked at one another as if they couldn't believe their ears.

"Us?" Kyler said in amazement. "You want *us* to take off ours?"

"So Candice won't feel lonely," Fargo said.

The three of them guffawed mightily, with Grizz doubling over and slapping his tree-trunk thighs in hilarity.

A lot of the townsfolk were looking at Fargo as if he was loco. Once again, there were two exceptions.

Against the rear wall leaned a thin man who wore a buckskin shirt that, unlike Fargo's, didn't have whangs. His pants were ordinary britches, and instead of boots he wore moccasins. High on his right hip was a Tranter revolver, not a common model on the frontier. He wore the kind of high-crowned, short-brimmed hat that Indians liked but he didn't appear to have Indian blood in him. He had folded his arms across his chest and showed no fear whatsoever of the Hollisters.

The other exception was over by the left-hand wall. A black flat-crowned hat that gamblers favored crowned his head but he wasn't dressed like a gambler in a frock coat and high boots. He had on a store-brought shirt and pants, both dark blue, both well worn. He wore two pistols. Oddly, they were mismatched. On his right side was a Remington Beals Navy. On his left hip was a Smith & Wesson. His thumbs were hooked in his gun belt, and he seemed more amused than anything.

Fargo waited for the Hollisters to get the mirth out of their systems, and as Grizz straightened, he said, "We'll start with you."

Grizz got real serious real quick. Flushing with anger, he snarled, "You are the stupidest jackass I ever came across."

Fargo smiled. "You must not look in the mirror much."

Grizz squared his broad shoulders and flexed his thick fingers. "Mister, I am goin' to—"

"No," Rance said.

Grizz stopped flexing and looked at his brother in confusion. "What's that?"

"No, I said."

"You heard him," Grizz said, gesturing at Fargo. "We don't let anyone talk to us like he's done."

Rance's eyes had narrowed and he was studying Fargo with new interest. He glanced out the front window at the hitch rail and gave a slight start. "I'll be," he said.

"What the hell has gotten into you?" Kyler snapped.

"Do you recollect that time we were down to Fort Laramie," Rance said, not taking his eyes off Fargo, "and we got to jawin' with those fellers about gunmen and man-killers and such?"

"What about it?" Kyler said.

"They talked about a gambler they'd heard of who had shot five men and a marshal who is quick on the shoot and that Captain Davis who kilt those ten or eleven bandits. You remember?"

"So the hell what?" Kyler said.

"So they told us about another feller," Rance said. "A scout, he was. Big man, hard as nails, who's killed a heap of gents."

"I sort of remember it," Kyler said. "So?"

"One of those fellers mentioned you can tell this scout by the horse he rides. A handsome pinto or some such." Rance bobbed his head at the front window. "Look out yonder and tell me what you see at the hitch rail."

Kyler and Grizz both looked, and Kyler said, "Well, I'll be."

"You're him, ain't you?" Rance said to Fargo. "The man-killin' scout?"

Fargo had never been called a man-killer before. Yes, he'd shot more than few, but always in self-defense, or to protect others. He didn't go out and look for men to kill.

Life just kept throwing them at him.

"You don't want to say?" Rance said. "That's fine. We got no quarrel with you, mister. We'll take our leave now."

"We'll what?" Grizz said.

Rance took a step toward the batwings, saying, "You heard me, brothers. Our frolic is over."

"No," Fargo said.

Rance stopped. "Why not?" he uneasily asked.

"Candice."

"What's she to you? Do you know her personal?"

"Never met her until today."

"My brother is drunk. He didn't know what he was doin'."

"Who are you talkin' about?" Grizz asked.

"You," Kyler said.

"What did I do?"

"You hit that dove."

"Oh. I forgot."

Rance had lowered a hand from the Sharps and tilted the muzzle at the ceiling. "You can see how he is, mister. How about if I have him say he's sorry and we call it even?"

"All your weapons on the floor," Fargo said, "or use them."

Rance's jaw muscles twitched but he slowly tucked at the knees and held his Sharps out in one hand to show he wasn't going to use it.

Kyler was flabbergasted. "What the hell are you doin'?"

"Keepin' us from bein' killed." Rance carefully set it down and straightened.

"You're eatin' crow, is what you're doin'," Kyler said in disgust.

Rance glared at him. "Little brother, shut the hell up. That Sharps ain't no feather. He'd put three or four slugs into me before I could point it."

"Now you, boy," Fargo said. "The knife."

Kyler swept his hand to the hilt and took a half step as if he intended to try to use it. But it must have occurred to him that he couldn't cover the fifteen feet that separated them before he was gunned down in his tracks. With an angry oath, he yanked the knife out and let it drop.

That left Grizz.

"Your turn," Fargo said, "and then we'll get to it."

"Get to what?" Grizz said. He looked at Rance, his brow furrowed. "What do I do? Do I shoot him or stab him or what?"

"You'd be dead before you cleared your belt. Just do as he says."

"I don't like this," Grizz said. "I don't like this at all." But he jerked his six-shooter and bowie and placed them at his feet. "Now what?"

"Now I beat the hell out of you," Fargo said.

4

It had begun to sink in to those along the walls that the worst of the danger was over. Low murmurs broke out and a few drifted toward the overturned tables.

Grizz's face was scrunched up as if he was in the outhouse and couldn't. "*You* are fixin' to beat *me*?"

Fargo pried at his buckle with his left hand, careful to keep his right hand close to his holster.

"With your fists?" Kyler said, and laughed.

Rance appeared perplexed. "I don't savvy you, mister. My brother will break you like a twig. And for what? A gal you don't even know."

"You two are to stay out of it," Fargo said.

Rance looked down at his Sharps, and slyly smiled. "Why, sure, mister. Whatever you say."

Spurs jingled behind Fargo, and the man with the black hat and mismatched revolvers came up on Fargo's right. His thumbs were still hooked in his gun belt. "I'll make sure they do."

"Who the hell are you?" Rance said.

"Handle's Crown," the man answered. "Rafer Crown."

Fargo had heard of him. Crown made his living hunting men for bounty money. He'd also been involved in a few shooting affrays and was considered a bad hombre to trifle with.

"What's this to you that you're stickin' your nose in?" Rance said.

"It interests me," Crown said.

"You didn't say nothin' when we were havin' our fun with that dove."

Crown shrugged. "Don't know her. No stake in it."

The next moment the man in the buckskin shirt was on Fargo's other side. He'd come up so silently, Fargo hadn't heard him. "I'd like to see this be a fair fight, too."

"What the hell?" Rance said. "And who are you?"

"Dirk Peters. I'm not as famous as Fargo, here, but I've done some scouting and tracking, and now and then, I shoot bastards like you three."

"You talk big now," Rance said, "but I didn't hear a peep before."

"You had that cannon trained on us," Dirk Peters said. "And my ma didn't raise no simpletons."

Fargo held out his gun belt to Peters. "I'd be obliged if you'd look after this."

Rafer Crown finally unhooked a thumb and jabbed it at Rance and Kyler. "You two, over by the window. Keep your hands where I can see them."

"And if we don't?" Kyler snarled.

Crown's hand flicked, and the Remington was in it. Everyone heard the *click* of the hammer. "I'm not this gent next to me. I don't care about fair. Sass me, I'll gun you. Cuss me, I'll gun you. You don't get your asses over by the window, I'll gun you."

Rance went to say something but closed his mouth and motioned for his younger brother to follow him to the window. "Will this do, you—" He caught himself before he finished.

Rafer Crown twirled the Remington into his holster as slick as could be. "Stay over there and behave." He looked at Fargo. "The dumb one is all yours."

Dirk Peters pointed at a couple of townsmen. "You two, scoot over and put their weapons on the bar."

"Why us?" one of them replied.

"Because I said so."

Reluctantly, the pair edged forward. They were scared to death of Grizz, and when they snatched his revolver and bowie, moved quickly to one side to get out of his reach.

Fargo stepped around a table and a chair and planted himself. "You hit that girl for not sitting in your lap?"

Grizz still seemed confused. He was slow to digest what was going on, and he made no move to defend himself. "That was part of it."

"What was the other part?"

"I hankered after a kiss and she wouldn't give me one."

"So you beat her and ripped her clothes off?"

"I only hit her once," Grizz said. "That's all it ever takes." He bunched his huge fists. "You're thinkin' you should punish me, is that it? That if you hurt me it'll teach me to be nicer?"

"I doubt you know what nice is."

"My pa used to think like you. When I was little, he'd take me out to the woodshed when I acted up. And I acted up a lot. But do you know what?"

Fargo didn't respond.

"It didn't change me none. And when I was big enough, I took that stick from him and broke it in half and beat him with it."

Fargo began to suspect that the hulking brute wasn't quite as dumb as he appeared.

"My ma used to say they had a word for me. Vicious, it was. She called me the most vicious boy who was ever born."

Grizz chuckled. "I broke her nose the last time she called me that."

"Your own parents," Dirk Peters said.

Grizz ignored him and glowered at Fargo. "What I did to that bitch in the street is nothin' to what I'm goin' to do to you. I'll break your bones and have you spittin' teeth."

In the back of Fargo's mind a tiny voice asked why he was doing this. They were right. He didn't know the girl. He had no personal stake, as Rafer Crown put it. But he never had been able to look the other way when an innocent was mistreated. It always stirred an anger in him.

That, and he had a vicious streak of his own. There were few things he liked more than to dose out a taste of their own medicine to sons of bitches like this Grizz.

"Nothin' to say? Cat got your tongue? Or is it you're afraid?"

"Of you?" Fargo snorted.

"Any last words?" Grizz asked.

"Is there a sawbones in this town?"

"Not that I know of," Grizz said. "Why?"

"You're going to need one."

5

Grizz lumbered toward Fargo, saying, "Do you know why they call me Grizz?"

"It's a common name for lumps of stupid," Fargo said.

And then there was no more talking.

Grizz waded in, his knobby fists raised in an awkward boxing stance. He flung an overhand that Fargo easily ducked. Quickly, Fargo retaliated with two jolts to the ribs that would have knocked other men onto their toes. All Grizz did was grunt.

Fargo sideslipped a jab and rammed a solid right to Grizz's jaw. Grizz's head barely moved an inch. A huge fist drove at Fargo's face and he got his left up to block it. Even so, the force of the blow sent him back on his bootheels and sent pain flaring down his arm to his toes.

Fargo realized this wasn't going to be a short fight.

Grizz was as strong as the proverbial ox. So what if Grizz possessed little skill. His enormous strength made up for it.

The wisest tactic for Fargo to adopt was to wear Grizz down. He slammed a straight-arm to Grizz's jaw, avoided an uppercut, and delivered a punch to the gut that would have folded most men in half.

Grizz grimaced.

A looping left knocked Fargo's hat off. Fargo landed good blows to Grizz's cheek, his side, his ear.

Red in the face with anger and frustration, Grizz roared, "Stand still!" He lunged with his arms spread wide.

Fargo sprang aside. Or tried to. He'd forgotten about the overturned tables and chairs and his boot caught on one of the latter. He tried to wrench free but crashed onto his back on the floor.

Grizz pounced. Grinning, he raised his leg and stomped his big boot down at Fargo's face. Fargo rolled, twisted, kicked Grizz in the knee and in the shin, and was on his feet before Grizz set himself.

Grizz bent and went to pick up the chair but stopped when a gun hammer clicked.

"No," Rafer Crown said.

Grizz glared at the bounty hunter but dropped the chair. "After I'm done with this jackrabbit, how about I pound you."

"I don't fight with fists," Crown said. "Only pistols." He smiled. "And anytime you reckon you're fast enough, I'll splatter your brains."

"You think you're somethin'," Grizz said.

From over at the window Rance hollered, "Forget about him, damn you, and take care of the scout."

Grizz turned. He raised his fists higher and hunched his thick shoulders and advanced.

Fargo unleashed everything he had. Jabs, uppercuts, rights, lefts, from the sides, from the front. Never still, always hitting. Grizz threw one punch to ten of his. But it was like beating on an adobe wall. It had no effect other than to make Grizz madder.

Fargo was growing winded. Instead of wearing Grizz down, he was wearing himself down. He backed off to gain a breather and those animal eyes of Grizz's glittered. Grizz knew.

"You're not so much," Grizz said.

The hell of it was, so far Fargo hadn't been. He set himself and for a minute they swapped blows and blocks and then he had to step back again.

"Won't be long now," Grizz crowed.

Fargo had to find a weakness, and quick. He decided to pick one spot and concentrate on that. The ribs wouldn't do. They were like iron bars. Grizz's gut wasn't much softer. Grizz's legs were redwoods. That left from the neck up.

Darting in, Fargo threw all he had in a swing to Grizz's jaw. It didn't have much more effect than the last one. Ducking, Fargo connected with another and then a third.

Now it was Grizz who stepped back. He shook his head and moved his jaw back and forth. "What are you tryin' to do?" he growled. "Break it?"

"Yes," Fargo said. He feinted, and when Grizz brought both hams in front of his face to protect it, Fargo tromped on Grizz's toes with his boot.

Grizz bellowed and lowered his hands.

Instantly, Fargo let loose with an uppercut. It caught Grizz flush under the jaw and rocked his head back. Grizz took an unsteady step back, the first weakness he'd shown.

Fargo went after him, Grizz's jaw his target. He was clipped on the shoulder but drove in three jabs to the chin. Despite Grizz's matting of heavy beard, each one jarred him.

The saloon was so quiet, you could have heard a pin drop.

Fargo glimpsed Rance and Kyler out of the corner of his eye. Rance looked worried.

The townsfolk were gawking in fascination. Fisticuffs were rare. West of the Mississippi, most disagreements were settled with gun smoke.

Grizz shook himself again, and now his eyes were pits of rage. With an inarticulate cry, he hurled himself at Fargo, his arms flung as wide as they would go.

Fargo retreated, collided with a table, and was brought to a stop.

The next moment Grizz had him.

6

It was like being caught in a giant vise.

Steel bands wrapped around Fargo's arms, pinning them. He struggled as Grizz lifted him bodily off the floor, and squeezed.

The pain was excruciating. It filled Fargo's chest, numbed his arms, blurred his vision.

Grizz laughed. "Got you now," he gloated. "Got you good as dead."

Fargo grit his teeth and twisted and kicked. With someone as immensely strong as Grizz, a bear hug could prove fatal. He needed to break free before his ribs gave under the pressure. They'd fracture and break and maybe puncture a lung.

Over at the window, Rance was laughing too. Kyler let out a whoop of joy.

Fargo couldn't pry loose, couldn't get leverage. In desperation he tried to drive his knee into Grizz's groin.

He heard himself gasp. He saw Grizz's chin swimming before him, and in fury slammed his forehead into it. To his surprise, it cleared his sight. He did it again and again and yet once more.

Grizz swayed.

Fargo's forehead was pure torment but he smashed it into Grizz's jaw two more times.

Grizz tottered and his grip weakened slightly. Not much but it fired Fargo with hope. He tucked his chin to his chest and slammed his head up under Grizz's jaw. There was a sharp crack and the crunch of teeth and Grizz howled and cast him to the floor.

Scrambling out of reach, Fargo regained his feet. His arms were tingling but he could use them. He countered a weak jab and kicked Grizz in the knee.

Grizz cursed, and his leg partly buckled. It brought his chin lower.

Now! Fargo thought. He whipped into an uppercut that snapped Grizz's head toward the ceiling. Once. Twice. And a third uppercut that left his hand hurting like hell—and brought Grizz crashing to the floor.

Fargo didn't know who was more surprised, him or the onlookers. He waited, his fists hiked, for Grizz to get up and renew their fight, but Grizz lay still, spittle flecking his mouth.

"Well," Fargo said.

Behind him, someone let out a long breath.

"You did it, by God," a townsman said.

Fargo's whole body was a welter of pain. He was barely aware when someone shoved something into his hand.

"You'll be wanting your six-shooter back," Dirk Peters said.

Fargo looked down at his holster. He drew his Colt and gave it a twirl and turned to the pair at the window. "Get over here."

Rance was boiling with hate. Kyler stared at Grizz in disbelief.

"What do you want now?" Rance snapped.

"Strip him."

"What?"

"You heard me," Fargo said. "Take off his clothes and leave them in a pile."

"Why in hell—" Rance began, and stopped. "Oh. I savvy. For the damn girl."

Fargo pointed the Colt. "You don't have all day."

They set to it, Kyler saying, "Grizz will by-God kill you for this, mister."

"He's welcome to try."

It took some doing. Grizz was so heavy, they had to work together, lifting him and rolling him so they could peel his shirt and pants. Tugging off his boots was a feat in itself. But at last they were done.

"What now, bastard," Rance snarled.

"Tote him out and light a shuck."

"We won't forget you for this," Rance vowed.

Each grabbed a huge arm. Bodies straining, they dragged their brother toward the batwings.

The saloon stayed still until Grizz had been pushed and shoved over a horse and Rance and Kyler climbed on theirs and Rance led the third animal off by the reins.

Then whoops and hollers broke out.

A small man in an apron came over. "I'll remember this all my born days. Would you care for a drink, mister?"

"I sure as hell would," Fargo said. His throat was parched.

"Coming right up. It's on the house for what you did for Candice."

That reminded Fargo. "Bring a blanket if you have it."

"What?" the bartender said. Then, "Oh. Sure. I have one in the back."

A gray-haired townsman approached and offered Fargo his hand, saying, "Mister, you have done us a favor. Those three have been the terrors of the territory for some spell now."

"I wish you'd just shot them," said someone else.

Fargo turned and offered his own hand to Dirk Peters. "I'm obliged for the help."

"Hell, it wasn't nothing," Dirk said.

Fargo did the same to Rafer Crown, saying, "Heard tell of you down to Denver."

"Heard of you all over," Crown said.

"Are you here after the bounty, too?" Dirk Peters asked.

"I don't hunt men for money," Fargo said. Which wasn't entirely true. He'd done it a couple of times but would never take it up as a profession. He liked scouting too much.

"Who said anything about a man?" Dirk Peters said, and chuckled.

"This bounty is for a bull," Rafer Crown said.

Fargo wasn't sure he'd heard right. "A what?"

"A bull," Crown repeated himself.

"The most valuable in the country, or damn near," Dirk Peters said.

Before Fargo could ask them to explain, the bartender returned with a blanket and a bottle of Monongahela.

"I reckoned this would do you better than a glass."

"You reckoned right," Fargo said. He took both and wheeled to go but the bartender had more to say.

"One more thing. That Rance Hollister doesn't own just one Sharps. He totes two on his saddle, one on either side."

Fargo had never heard of anyone doing that.

The bartender went on. "It wouldn't surprise me none if he only went a short way and is out there waiting to pick you off."

"Hell," Fargo said.

7

Fargo poked his head over the batwings and looked both ways. The street was still deserted expect for the forlorn naked figure a block away.

A cloud of dust to the west assured him that the three brothers were, in fact, gone.

Still, Fargo hugged the buildings until he was almost to Candice and then crossed to her and spread the blanket.

Her head was bowed, her hair over her face as before. She started when he draped the blanket over her shoulders and stiffened in alarm.

"It's only me," Fargo said. "You're safe now."

"You shouldn't," Candice said. "The one who did this to me—"

"They're gone."

"Oh," Candice said. "I heard horses but I didn't look."

Fargo parted her hair. Her swollen eye was worse, her cheek a dark black and blue.

"Did you have anything to do with their leaving?"

"I did," Fargo said.

Candice managed a smile. "I don't think I ever caught your name."

Fargo told her and held up the bottle. "Care for some firewater?"

"I damn well would."

Fargo opened it and offered it to her. She didn't take just a sip. She tilted it and gulped. A third of the bottle was gone when she handed it back.

"I'm grateful."

"Hell, woman," Fargo said. "You did know that's whiskey and not water?"

Candice laughed, and winced. "It never affects me for some reason. I can drink all day and all night and never get drunk."

"We must be twins."

She laughed again, and a lot of the tension and misery drained away. "Listen to you, Skye Fargo. You are my new favorite person."

"How about I get you back to the saloon?"

"Wearing a blanket? Hell no. How about you take me to my place. It's just up the street a ways."

"Need a hand?"

"No."

Fargo noticed that she sagged and moved stiffly so he put his arm around her anyway. "Here," he said.

Candice fixed her good eye on him. "Why are you being so nice?"

"I like your tits."

She snickered, then snorted, then burst out laughing and stopped herself to say, "Damn you. Don't do that. It hurts when I laugh."

"Don't do what? Like your tits?"

Candice did more laughing, only softer, and leaned into him. "Damn, my face hurts like hell."

"Maybe you shouldn't talk, then."

"No, that's all right." She paused. "So why *are* you being so nice? No one else helped. The men in this town have as much backbone as oatmeal. And the others here for the bounty didn't butt in, either."

"There's that word again," Fargo said.

"Which?"

"Bounty."

Candice tilted her face to him. "Isn't that why you're here?"

"I was just passing through."

"Oh my. And you came to the aid of a poor, defenseless maiden. Just like that Ivanhoe in that book."

"I'm not a knight in shining armor," Fargo said flatly.

"What are you then?"

"Randy," Fargo said.

Candice tried to stop herself from laughing but couldn't. "Damn you. Will you cut that out?" She took a deep breath. "Take a right at the next corner. We're almost there."

Fargo had glimpsed faces peering out at them from the windows of businesses and homes.

Candice saw them, too. "Bunch of rabbits. Although I suppose I can't blame them. Those Hollisters are as mean as anything." She leaned against him even more, until he was supporting most of her weight.

"Do you need me to carry you?" Fargo asked. He admired her grit almost as much as he admired her tits.

"I'm tuckered out, is all," Candice said. But that didn't stop her from saying, "That bounty I mentioned is for a bull. There's a man, Jim Tyler. He started up the first cattle ranch in these parts about, oh, a year or so ago. A couple of months back he brought in a stud bull all the way from Texas. He paid twenty thousand dollars for it, or so folks say."

Fargo whistled.

"I know. That's more than most folks make in a lifetime. But now the bull has gone missing and Tyler is beside himself. He thinks it wandered off into the mountains. If he can't find it he's out all that money, and from what I hear, he doesn't have enough to buy another. So he's doing the next best thing."

"Which is?"

"Offering a bounty to anyone who finds his bull and brings it back safe and sound. You should give it a try."

"It would take a heap of money to get me to go after some bull," Fargo said. "How much bounty are we talking about?"

"Five thousand dollars."

Fargo whistled again.

"Is that heap enough for you?"

Fargo thought of the whiskey he could buy and the doves he could treat himself to and the poker games he could sit in on, and had to admit, "It just might be."

8

Her room was in a boardinghouse, at the rear. She asked him to take her in the back way so no one would see her face.

Fargo obliged her. He knew how some women were about their looks. No one was in the hall and he slipped her into her room and over to her bed. He went to ease her down but the moment he loosened his hold, she collapsed onto her side.

Candice groaned and uttered a slight sound, as if she might break into tears.

"You all right?"

"Be back on my feet in no time," Candice said with her good eye closed.

"Anything I can fetch you?"

"All I want now is to sleep."

Fargo turned to leave but she suddenly showed some life and snatched his hand.

"I want to thank you, again, for what you did. It was sweet."

"I'm many things," Fargo said, "but not that."

"Still." Candice mustered a lopsided smile. The half of her face that was swollen wouldn't move. "When I'm up to it, and if you're still around, I'll treat you to a night you won't forget."

"Night, hell," Fargo said with a grin. "How about a week?"

"Deal," Candice said. She began to laugh, winced in pain, and closed her eye again. "I'll ride you until you chafe," she said softly, and passed out.

Fargo touched her hair. "Quite a gal," he said. He left quietly. In the hall he paused. Instead of turning to the back door, he walked to the front of the house.

A parlor on the left was occupied by a man and a woman in their middle years. The woman was in a chair, tense with fear. The man was staring out the front window and jumped when Fargo said, "Folks."

"Who are you?" the man demanded in a tone that told Fargo he was more mouse than lion. "What are you doing in here?"

"You run this boardinghouse?" Fargo asked.

"We both do," the woman said. "Harold works at the general store but this gives us extra money."

"The woman, Candice . . ." Fargo began.

"Candice Phelps," the woman said.

"She was beat by the Hollisters. She's in her room, hurt bad."

"Oh God," Harold said. "I was sent home and Mr. Ogilby closed the store, he's so scared of them."

"Seems to be a lot of that going around." Fargo focused on the woman. "I hear there's no doc in this town."

"There isn't," she confirmed.

"Candice is asleep now but in a few hours you should look in on her."

"Don't you worry. I like Candice. We'll take real good care of her."

To the man Fargo said, "You can stop trembling. The Hollisters have left."

"Thank God," the man said. "It's a wonder they didn't kill anybody."

Fargo touched his hat brim to the woman and left by the front door. The sudden glare of the afternoon sun after the half shadow of the house made him squint. He turned up the street and happened to gaze its full length to the prairie beyond.

A flash of light gleamed far off.

Fargo flung himself at the ground. Hardly had he done so when something whistled over his head. The distant boom of the shot followed half a second later.

Rance Hollister was out there with his Sharps.

In the hands of a marksman, a Sharps could hit a target from half a mile off. But it was a single-shot and took a few seconds to reload.

Rolling, Fargo heaved up and ran between two buildings before Hollister could get off another. Hot fury boiled in his veins. The Hollisters would have been smart to leave it be. Now he couldn't just ride off.

Staying out of the open, Fargo reached the saloon.

Nearly everyone was drinking and talking excitedly and a couple of card games had resumed. They were making so much noise, no one had heard the shot.

The place fell as silent as a cemetery when Fargo strode in.

Rafer Crown and Dirk Peters were at a corner table, and Peters beckoned.

The bartender had just brought a couple of glasses over for them.

Going over, Fargo pulled out a chair and set down his bottle. "I'm obliged for the warning about Rance."

"He tried?" the barman asked.

"He did."

"They won't give up, you know," the bartender said. "I put the rest of their weapons in the back room if you want them."

"I don't."

The bartender shrugged and returned to the bar.

"If it was me," Rafer Crown said, "I'd gun them on sight the next time I see them. Whether they are heeled or not."

Fargo chugged and let out an "Ahhh" at the welcome burning that spread from his throat to his belly. "I take it you gents are going after the bull?"

Dirk Peters nodded. "The hunt commences tomorrow. That rancher, Jim Tyler, sent circulars all over about a month ago. I saw one in Utah."

"It was Denver for me," Crown said.

"There's a lot of others who have shown up," Dirk Peters said. "We're to meet at Tyler's spread tomorrow morning at ten."

"Why all at once?" Fargo asked.

Dirk shrugged. "Tyler's idea. Word is he's got something he wants to say to those who go after the critter."

"Sounds like a waste of time to me," Rafer Crown said. "I'd have been off hunting it by now."

"From man hunter to bull hunter," Dirk Peters said with a grin.

"For five thousand dollars I'd hunt a damn frog," Crown said.

"How long has this bull been missing?" Fargo wanted to know.

"About two months," Dirk Peters said.

Fargo took another swallow. "It could be dead by now. Or clear up in Canada." He was only joking about that last but the bull might have wandered anywhere.

"Word is that a couple of trappers spotted Thunderhead about two weeks ago not ten miles from the ranch house," Dirk Peters revealed.

"Thunderhead? Tyler gave the bull a name?"

"He probably thinks it's one of the family," Dirk joshed.

"Why didn't the trappers bring it back for the reward?" Fargo asked.

"They tried, but the bull didn't want to come," the bounty hunter said.

"They lost a packhorse for their trouble and nearly got gored, besides," Dirk said.

"So Thunderhead is no kitten," Fargo said.

"More monster than cat," Dirk declared. "Half the size of a stagecoach, or so folks claim. With horns out to here." He spread his arms as wide as they would go. "And the temper of a rabid wolf."

"Hell," Fargo said.

"Yes, sir," Dirk Peters said. "Any gent who goes after Thunderhead is taking his life in his hands."

9

Fargo mulled that over the rest of the day.

Both Crown and Peters could track, and with them after the bounty, finding the bull first wasn't a sure thing.

He entertained second thoughts about joining the hunt. But there was Candice's promise of delights to come, and the Hollister brothers to deal with.

Fargo decided he might as well try while he waited for her to heal and for him to have his chance at the Hollisters.

His bottle was almost empty when he sat in on a poker game.

The townsmen seemed in awe of him. That anyone had had the sand to stand up to the Hollisters, especially Grizz, was a wonderment. Many wanted to shake his hand and thank him. And more than a few were eager to sit in on the game.

Fargo was happy to have them. Nearly all were piss-poor players and he liked taking their money.

By eleven or so that night, fatigue started to set in. Fargo raked in his winnings and added them to his poke and rose. "This is it for me, gents," he announced.

Crown and Peters were already gone.

Fargo nodded to a few townsmen who had been particularly friendly, and pushed on the batwings. A breath of cool night air fanned him.

Fargo stepped from under the overhang and bent to unwrap the reins just as the Ovaro raised its head and looked above him. Simultaneously, there came a scraping sound from the overhang.

Instinct propelled Fargo into whirling and going for his Colt just as a dark form smashed into his chest. Knocked back, he lost his hold on the revolver.

Cold steel flashed in the light from the saloon window, nearly taking out an eye.

Backpedaling, Fargo saw who it was.

"I've got you now, you son of a bitch," Kyler Hollister gloated. He wagged his antler-handled knife and grinned in glee. "Rance didn't want me to come but I snuck off and here I am."

Fargo realized Kyler must have ventured into the back of the saloon and found their weapons. "I'm glad you did."

"Glad?" Kyler said.

"One less of you I have to track down."

"I by-God can't wait to kill you." Kyler came on in a crouch, his knife held in a way that told Fargo he knew how to use it. "For what you did to Grizz, I aim to make you suffer."

"Talking me to death is a good start."

Kyler hissed and attacked. He thrust high, slashed low, and hissed again when Fargo avoided both. "I forgot how quick you are."

"Quicker than you Hollisters," Fargo goaded as his hand dipped to his boot. In the partial dark the youngest Hollister didn't notice. "Being turtles must run in your family."

"I'll show you turtle," Kyler growled, and closed.

By then Fargo had the Arkansas toothpick out. He parried, and at the ring of steel on steel, Kyler uttered an oath and leaped back.

"So you have a blade too."

Fargo grinned.

"That little splinter against my big knife?" Kyler said. "I'll cut you to ribbons."

"You jabber as much as a girl."

That did it. Kyler swore and attacked, and while he wasn't the best knife fighter Fargo had ever tangled with, the boy was good, damn good, and damn deadly, and it was all Fargo could do to stay alive.

They thrust, they stabbed, they circled. Every move was countered. Kyler was a lot smaller, but he was a rattler on two legs.

Fargo had been in enough fights to know that the longer it lasted, the more likely it was that he'd be cut or worse. He had to end it fast. But try as he might, he couldn't get the toothpick past that oversized blade of Kyler's.

The boy grew cocky. He laughed. He smirked. When Fargo tried a cut to the neck that he nimbly evaded, Kyler chuckled and said, "You're not so much, mister. You stood up to Grizz and knocked him out but you won't get the better of me."

"Says the infant," Fargo said.

"Your goadin' won't work anymore," Kyler said, dipping low to the ground. "I'm serious now, and you're dead."

Poised on the balls of his feet, Fargo crouched, ready for anything. Or so he thought. The next moment, Kyler flung a handful of dust at his face. Fargo brought his hand up but some of the dust flew into his eyes.

And suddenly he couldn't see.

10

The world became a blur.

Fargo backpedaled and swiped at his eyes with a sleeve but Kyler Hollister was a vague shape and nothing more. He heard Hollister laugh and felt a sting in his arm.

Fargo was in trouble. He kept on retreating and blinking. They were in the middle of the street where the light barely reached.

Kyler lanced that long knife at Fargo's belly, and with a hairs-breadth to spare, Fargo sidestepped and continued to put distance between them.

"You can't avoid me much longer, mister."

The hell of it was, the boy was right. Fargo still couldn't see. He was a blind goat waiting to be slaughtered.

Just then the batwings opened and out of the saloon came four townsmen who drew up short.

"Look there!" one shouted.

"It's that Hollister kid!" another exclaimed.

"What do you think you're doing?" a third hollered.

Kyler did the last thing Fargo expected. He swore and bolted.

"After him!" one of the townsmen shouted but no one gave chase.

Fargo furiously wiped at his eyes. Another blink, and his sight was back.

Kyler Hollister had disappeared into the night. Chasing him would be pointless.

Sliding the toothpick into its ankle sheath, Fargo unfurled and turned to his saviors. "I'm obliged, gents."

"What did we do?" the first man asked.

"You saved my hash," Fargo said. Fishing his poke out, he loosened the drawstring and plucked a coin and tossed it and one of them caught it.

"Why, it's a ten-dollar gold piece."

"Treat yourselves."

They looked at one another and then at the ten-dollar coin.

"We could buy a whole bottle," one said.

"Hell, we could buy two," said another.

"I didn't really want to go home anyhow," remarked a third.

"A bottle it is, then."

Laughing and clapping one another on the back, they reentered the saloon. Right before the batwings closed, one of them thought to holler, "Thanks, mister."

Fargo was the one who should thank them. That dust in the face almost did him in. He reclaimed his Colt.

Climbing on the Ovaro, he reined to an alley and along it until he came to the prairie. He supposed he could go ask if there was a room at the boardinghouse but it was late and he was tired and sore as hell from his fight with Grizz.

And now Fargo had something new he owed the Hollister brothers for.

Dappled by starlight and a sliver of moon, he rode until he came on a dry wash. It would shunt most of the wind and hide him from unfriendly eyes.

Riding down into it, Fargo dismounted. He stripped the Ovaro, spread out his bedroll, and lay on his back with his saddle for a pillow.

Overhead, a myriad of stars speckled the firmament. He never saw this many when he was in a city or town. Only in the wilds, where the skies were clear as crystal and there were no lights to interfere.

Fargo thought about the missing bull. The five thousand was too much to pass up. Maybe he'd find it and maybe he wouldn't. All it would cost him was a few days. A week at the most, he reckoned.

Where others might rest fitfully after the day he'd had, Fargo slept soundly until the stamp of the Ovaro's hoof ended his slumber. Feeling sluggish and drowsy, he rose onto his elbows.

Dawn was on the cusp of turning the eastern sky pink, and the stallion was staring intently to the south.

Jamming his hat on, Fargo cast off his blanket and crept to the top of the wash.

A lone rider was making for town along the ribbon of road.

"You're turning into a worrier," he said to the stallion, and set about throwing his saddle blanket on and saddling up.

Fargo liked to start his day with coffee and recollected a restaurant that had a sign in the window advertising "the best breakfasts this side of the Divide." He was skeptical of the claim but he did like the idea of having food served to him rather than making it himself. He was on the go so much, he grew tired of his own cooking.

By the time he got there the sun was up.

Most of the dozen or so customers stopped eating to stare. Evidently words of his clash with the Hollisters had spread.

Fargo paid them no mind. It was a new day and he'd start it right. When a gray-haired woman in an apron came for his order, he asked for six eggs, scrambled, two slices of toast with butter and jam, enough bacon to "gag a horse," and for her to keep the coffee coming until it poured out his ears.

"A gent who likes to eat," she said, chuckling. "You're a customer after my own heart."

The coffee was delicious. Fargo was on his second cup, and his meal had yet to show, when the door opened and in ambled Rafer Crown and Dirk Peters. Peters spotted him and they came over.

"Mind if we join you?" Crown asked.

"It's a big table," Fargo said.

"We're on our way out to the Tyler spread as soon as we're finished," Dirk Peters mentioned. "Care to join us?"

"Might as well."

Rafer Crown sat so his right hand was close to his Navy.

"There's a rumor going around that you were in a knife fight after we left you last night."

"Wasn't much of a fight," Fargo said.

"The rumor says it was Kyler Hollister," Dirk Peters said.

"It was."

"That's the thing with these Hollisters, we hear," Dirk said. "Rile them, and they keep coming at you until you're dead."

"Worth keeping in mind," Rafer Crown remarked.

"It surely is," Fargo said.

11

The Tyler ranch was five miles out of town, situated along the foothills that served as stairs to the high country. It consisted of a house, a stable, a bunkhouse and a chicken coop.

The rancher was on his porch with a couple of his cowhands and a woman who must have been his wife.

Fargo was mildly surprised to see that nearly twenty people had gathered to hear what Jim Tyler had to say. And he wasn't the only one.

"I didn't expect this many," Rafer Crown said.

"The five thousand has brought them out of the woodwork," Dirk Peters said.

"Look at them," the bounty hunter grumbled. "Most couldn't find their asses without help."

Fargo was looking, and he was inclined to agree.

There was an old woman, pushing seventy if she was a day, in a bonnet and dress, armed with a Colt Dragoon, of all things, strapped tight around her waist. The Dragoon was so heavy, her holster sagged halfway to her knees.

There were three kids on their own, the oldest not more than twelve or thirteen, all with freckles and red hair and squirrel rifles.

There was a young man and woman in smart city clothes who looked enough alike to be brother and sister. She was twirling a parasol and he looked bored.

"God in heaven," Dirk Peters said.

"I need a drink," Crown muttered.

Fargo was still looking. He guessed that a big man in bib overalls was a farmer and that a pair of men in red caps and checkered shirts were loggers. Fully three-fourths were townsfolk who would be lucky if they could track themselves to the outhouse.

"Nothing to say?" Dirk Peters asked him, grinning.

"It's plumb ridiculous," Fargo said.

"Make that two drinks," Crown said.

Jim Tyler was supposed to kick things off at ten. It wasn't much past nine but he stepped to the porch rail and surveyed those who had gathered and seemed about as impressed as anyone with common sense would be. Then he set eyes on Fargo, Rafer Crown and Dirk Peters and gave a nod of approval.

"He knows we're not worthless," Crown said.

The rancher cleared his throat. "My name is Jim Tyler, as all of you surely know. This ranch you see around you is one of the first in the territory. I have high hopes for it. If I can make a go of raising livestock, others might try the same. Ten years from now, a lot of folks could be making their living off cattle, just like in Texas and Kansas and elsewhere."

"Bet he's one of those long-winded cusses," Dirk Peters said.

Tyler continued. "I brought a herd all the way from Texas. They say I'm one of the first to do that. I also brought my prize bull. I call him Thunderhead because the day we got here, there was a gully-washer, and he was a sight standing there with his big horns and all while the rain poured down and lightning split the sky."

"Yep," Dirk said. "Long-winded as hell."

Tyler had paused and was grinning at a memory. "Getting Thunderhead here wasn't easy. He didn't want to come. He especially didn't like walking so far every day. So we tricked him. He was partial to a heifer my missus took to calling Mabel, and one of the hands led her by a rope and Thunderhead would follow. If not for her, we'd likely still be in Texas."

There was a smattering of laughter.

"I've treated that bull like he was part of the family. Had a special pen made. Gave him plenty of feed and care. Hell, I treat him as good as I treat my wife."

More polite laughter rippled.

"I can't tell you how important Thunderhead is to me. My whole future rests on him. He can mean the difference between my ranch succeeding or dying."

"An iffy proposition," Rafer Crown commented, "depending on cows for a living."

"Two months ago, as you've undoubtedly heard, Thunderhead disappeared. I came out to his pen one morning and he was gone. The gate got open. How, I don't know. I always made sure it was

33

shut at night. I feared it might be redskins. Blackfeet have been seen hereabouts a lot lately. But I couldn't find any sign of them. No moccasin prints, no tracks of unshod ponies, nothing."

"That's all we'd need," Dirk said.

Tyler's shoulders slumped. "I thought maybe Thunderhead had been rustled, but I couldn't see someone just leading him off. He'd put up a fuss."

"Could he have opened the gate his own self?" the man in the bib overalls hollered. "I had a cow that could do that."

"I suppose," Tyler said. "If he hooked his horn under the bar and lifted. But he never once tried to get out. He had it easy and I suspect he knew it."

"Did you try tracking him?" asked the old woman with the Colt Dragoon.

"I did, ma'am," Tyler answered. "I'm not much shakes at it but I tracked him into the mountains yonder and lost the sign."

Fargo gazed to the west where a rugged range formed an arc some seventy miles long. Beyond, and higher still, reared the stark backbone of the Rockies.

"I'm desperate," Tyler was saying. "Which is why I sent out the circulars some of you have seen. And why I'm offering five thousand dollars to have my bull back in his pen where he belongs." He surveyed those who had come. "If you want to go after him, fine. If you find him, the money is yours. But I should warn you. The mountains are no place for infants. If you're green to this, you shouldn't be going."

"He has that right," Dirk Peters said.

"There are grizzlies up there, and wolves, and more besides," the rancher said. "There are those Blackfeet I told you about, who will lift your hair as quick as look at you."

"Right about that, too," Dirk said.

"I don't want any of your lives on my conscience. If you've never hunted or tracked before, go home. The bounty isn't worth your life."

"It is to me," Rafer Crown said.

None of the listeners made a move for their mounts.

"Very well, then," Jim Tyler said. "It's on your heads. But I warn you one last time. A lot of you could well die."

12

After the rancher was done, Fargo went up and offered his hand.

Tyler looked at him and at Crown and Peters. "You three strike me as the best of the bunch."

"We should," Dirk Peters said.

"If your bull is still breathing," Rafer Crown said, "I'll find him."

"If I don't find him first," Dirk Peters said.

"I like gents with confidence," Tyler said. "You'll need it up there."

Just then the old woman wearing the Colt Dragoon came over. "Good to see you again, Jim."

"Esther," Tyler said. "What in God's name do you think you're doing?"

"My Charlie was a damn fine tracker and he taught me his tricks," Esther said. "I have as good a chance as any of these other idiots."

"Why are you looking at me, lady?" Dirk Peters asked.

"You have idiot written all over you."

"Here now," Dirk said.

"You're too old," Tyler bluntly told her.

"Old, hell," Esther retorted. "I've got more vinegar in me than you four peckerwoods put together."

"Lady, I don't like being insulted," Rafer Crown warned.

"What are you going to do? Shoot an old woman for speaking her mind?"

"Is it the money?" Tyler asked her.

"What else?"

"I liked your husband, Esther. He was a good man," Tyler said. "It's a shame the Lord took him to his reward and left you alone. You should go back east. Don't you have a daughter who lives in Missouri?"

"Hell, living with her would bore me to tears. I'm going after your bull and that's final." Esther smiled sweetly and walked off.

"Damn," Dirk Peters said. "That is one feisty gal."

"Feisty won't help her much with the Blackfeet," Rafer Crown said.

Now it was the farmer who approached, his thumbs hooked in his suspenders. "Mr. Tyler," he said with a nod of greeting.

"Humphries," Tyler said. "Shouldn't you be tending to your fields?"

"For five thousand dollars they can wait."

"You're worse than Esther," Tyler said.

"Worse how? Your bounty is more than I'd earn in ten years. I could have a bigger farmhouse built, treat my family to things."

"You can't if you're dead," Tyler said.

"I've hunted. I'm not helpless."

"I hope not, for your family's sake."

Humphries smiled at them and strolled away.

"What have I done?" Tyler said to himself. "These people are going to get themselves killed."

"You haven't seen anything yet," Dirk Peters said, gesturing.

The young couple in the smart city clothes approached, looking for all the world as if they were out for a Sunday stroll. The woman twirled her parasol, the young man ran a finger over his neatly trimmed mustache.

"Mr. Tyler," the young man said. "We wanted to make your acquaintance, my sister and I."

"Good God," Tyler said.

"Now, now," the young man said. "I'm Glyn Richmond and this is my sister, Aramone. Don't let our attire deceive you. My sister and I are more competent than you appear to think. She's a fine shot. She once bagged a squirrel at two hundred yards."

"A squirrel?" Dirk Peters said, and snorted.

"Squirrels don't claw you to pieces," Rafer Crown said. "Grizzlies do."

"I assure you, good sir," Glyn Richmond said, "we're prepared for anything."

"Does that include the Blackfeet?" Dirk Peters asked.

Aramone was eyeing Fargo. She ran her gaze from his hat to his boots and up again. "And who might you be, tall and silent?"

Fargo told her.

"You won't be disappointed, will you, handsome, if we beat you to the bull?" she teased.

"Sis," Glyn said.

"I'm only being friendly." Aramone twirled her parasol and winked at Fargo and they ambled off.

"The females fall right over you, don't they?" Dirk Peters said, and laughed.

"Must be nice," Rafer Crown said.

Jim Tyler wasn't the least bit amused. "They shouldn't be here. Nor most of the rest."

"They're grown-ups," Dirk said. "They can do as they please no matter how dumb it is."

"Not all of them are grown," Crown said. He was staring at the three redheaded boys.

"These Blackfeet," Fargo thought to bring up. "Is it a war party? And how many?"

"The word I got is that there's seven or eight," Tyler answered. "The hunter who saw them didn't say if they wore war paint or not."

"Doesn't matter if they do," Dirk Peters said. "They'd likely as not scalp any white they caught anyway."

"There's something else," Jim Tyler said, and lowered his voice. "Something I should have told everyone else, I reckon. It's about Thunderhead."

"Let me guess," Dirk Peters said. "He'll balk at being brought back."

"I figured as much but that won't stop me," Rafer Crown said.

"He'll do more than balk," Tyler informed them.

"What else can he do?" Dirk asked.

"Kill you."

"How's that again?"

"Thunderhead has gored three men to death."

13

To Fargo this bull hunt was getting better by the moment. First there were all the greenhorns. Then there were the Blackfeet. And now, "You're saying Thunderhead is a man-killer?"

Tyler nodded. "It's why the rancher in Texas was willing to sell him."

"Hell," Dirk Peters said.

"Two of the men he gored were trying to herd him into a pen," Tyler said. "For some reason he snapped and gored them. The third man was on the way here. One of my hands was trying to persuade him to ford a river and he brought down the hand and his horse."

"And you didn't think to tell everyone else?" Dirk said.

"I don't want them so scared of him that they shoot him if he acts up."

"I won't be gored," Rafer Crown said. "Your bull tries that with me, I'll put lead in his brainpan."

"See? Please, try not to," Tyler said. "I'm begging you."

"Better and better," Fargo said.

"How's that?"

Before Fargo could answer, a woman on the porch called to the rancher and he excused himself, saying simply, "It's the missus."

"What do you think?" Dirk Peters asked when the rancher was out of earshot.

"I'm right pleased," Crown said.

"Why?"

Crown motioned. "Most of these folks don't have a snowball's chance in hell of finding that critter. I can almost feel the money in my poke."

"Put the cart before the horse, why don't you?" Dirk said. "Any one of them could have a stroke of luck and find him."

"More likely they'll find an early grave."

The pair went on talking as Fargo made for a pump toward the side of the house. He worked the handle and after half a dozen tries water splashed out. Cupping his hand, he caught some and drank.

"How about a little for a lady, there, handsome?"

Fargo turned.

Aramone Richmond had closed her parasol and was holding it across a slender shoulder. She smiled and ran the tip of her tongue along her ruby lips. "I'm terribly thirsty."

"There's no cup," Fargo said.

"Who needs one?" she said, with a meaningful look.

Fargo pumped and cupped and held out his hand to her. Grinning, she pressed her lips to his palm and sipped, her eyes on his the whole time. When she was done, she flicked her tongue across his wet palm.

"That was nice of you."

"I can be nicer," Fargo said.

"Oh?"

"Come visit me sometime when your brother isn't around."

"Listen to you," Aramone said huskily. "What would you do if we were alone?"

"Screw you silly."

Where some women would be offended, Aramone laughed merrily. "Promises, promises," she said, and stared at his crotch. "You never know what might happen up in those mountains."

"Anytime," Fargo said.

With a saucy flip of her hips, Aramone sashayed toward her brother. She looked back and puckered her lips as if blowing Fargo a kiss.

"I'll be damned," Fargo said.

Over on the porch, Jim Tyler turned from his wife and raised his arms to get everyone's attention. "You're welcome to start hunting for Thunderhead anytime you want."

"Hold on, mister," a man called out. "What about those trappers who saw him? Where did they see him at?"

"About ten miles northwest of here."

"Anything else we need to know?" someone else asked.

Fargo expected the rancher to tell them about the gorings but Tyler shook his head.

"I wish each of you the best of luck. Thunderhead means everything to me. Whoever finds him will have my eternal thanks."

"I'd rather have the money," Humphries, the farmer, said, provoking more laughter.

Rafer Crown and Dirk Peters came to the pump.

"I reckon this is where we part company," Crown said. "From here on out it's every hombre for himself."

"We could work together," Dirk suggested. "Split the money three ways."

"No, thanks," Crown said. "Sixteen hundred dollars is a lot less than five thousand."

"With the Blackfeet on the prowl, we'd be better off."

"They don't worry me none," Crown said. "I've fought redskins before." He touched his hat brim and departed.

"Well, damn," Dirk said, and faced Fargo. "How about you? I'm willing to settle for half if you are."

It wasn't the money as far as Fargo was concerned. It was the fact he preferred to go it alone.

"Never mind," Dirk said. "I can tell by your face you're not interested, either. It must be my breath." He touched the brim of his high-crowned hat and left.

Fargo turned to go and found his way barred by Esther, the old gal with the Dragoon. She was giving him a strange sort of scrutiny. "Ma'am?" he said.

"You know," she said, "you look good enough to eat."

14

"A gal your age," Fargo joked. "You should be ashamed of yourself."

"A woman is never too old for *that*," Esther said. "And I've gone without since my Charlie died."

"Don't look at me."

"You don't like your women wrinkled like a prune?" Esther chuckled. "That's all right. I see myself in the mirror every day. I wouldn't hanker to give me a poke, either."

Fargo didn't know what to say to that.

"But I didn't come over to talk pokes. What do you say to the two of us partnering up? I cook better than most and I'll use this cannon if I have to." Esther patted the Colt Dragoon.

"Sorry. I like to ride alone."

"Too bad. Of all of them, I take you for the most trustworthy."

"You don't know me," Fargo said.

"True. But I read people real good. Comes from living so long. Oh, well." Esther smiled and made off toward Humphries.

"Enough of this," Fargo said. It was time to get the hell gone. And he wasn't the only one who thought so. Several would-be bounty hunters had peeled from the rest and climbed on their animals and gigged them toward the mountains.

Fargo bent his steps toward the Ovaro, only to have Jim Tyler call his name and beckon.

The rancher's wife was at his side. A mousy little thing, she was wringing her hands and giving the departing riders an anxious look.

"This is Clementine, my wife," Jim Tyler said. "She'd like a word with you."

"Oh?" Fargo said. It seemed like everyone wanted one.

"Jim has told me who you are," Clementine said. "That you've scouted for the army, and you have a reputation."

Fargo thought of all the women he'd bedded and the liquor he'd swilled and the countless nights of cards.

"I've never claimed to be a churchgoer."

"What? No. Jim tells me you're an honorable man."

Fargo figured the rancher must have him confused with some other scout. Or with Daniel Boone, maybe.

"He says you always do what's right."

Now Fargo was sure the rancher was mistaken. "I do what's right for me, ma'am." He almost added that he didn't much give a damn about anyone else.

"I'd like for you to do me a favor," Clementine said. "I'm willing to pay you out of my own purse for your trouble."

"I wish you wouldn't," Jim said. "There's no need."

"I say there is." Clementine took Fargo aback by clasping his hand. "You've seen these folks?" She indicated the dispersing riders, some with pack animals in tow. "What's your opinion of them?"

"They're pitiful," Fargo said.

"That's my assessment, too. I can't help but think that some of them won't make it back. And I wouldn't want that. It's our bull, after all."

"Clementine," Jim said.

"Hush. I have a right to do this and I will." She stared at the retreating figure of Esther on a mule. "Mr. Fargo, I'd like for you to look after them."

"Do what?"

"You heard right. I'm willing to pay you a hundred dollars of my own money if you'll keep an eye on them so they don't come to harm."

Fargo looked at Tyler.

"It wasn't my idea."

"It's mine," Clementine said. "A hundred dollars is no small amount. All you'd have to do is keep your eyes and ears peeled and if any of them get into trouble, you help them out."

Fargo didn't know where to begin. He tried with, "Ma'am, there are twenty or more. I can't keep watch over all of them."

"I'm not asking you to. I know you want to hunt for Thunderhead yourself. But as you're hunting, do what you can."

Jim Tyler frowned. "You're asking an awful lot of him, dear."

"I know." Clementine squeezed Fargo's hand and patted his arm. "I thank you from the bottom of my heart." She turned and stepped to the screen door and Jim opened it for her and they went in.

"Son of a bitch," Fargo said.

15

The range that Thunderhead had wandered off into didn't have a name yet. Neither did many of the rivers and streams and lakes. Much of the territory was unexplored, let alone settled.

Some would call it a subrange. The highest peaks, Fargo had heard, pushed two miles up, and seemed to brush the clouds.

Granite slabs and stretches of flat rock were everywhere. The forests were mostly pine but there were firs and aspens, too.

There were no towns and no settlements and, except for a few trappers and mountain men, no whites, either. The Blackfeet roamed it, as they had for who knew how long, and resented any and all intrusions.

Fargo had passed through the range several times in his many wanderings but didn't know it all that well.

Now, as he climbed the foothills, he pondered the state of affairs and wondered if he wasn't making a mistake.

First off, while Thunderhead was supposed to be an exceptionally large bull, finding him, when he had the entire range to hide in, was like looking for that well-known needle in a haystack.

Second, with over twenty bounty hunters searching, it would be luck more than anything for him to find it before anyone else. Granted, most were as green as grass and had no business being there, but greed always brought out the stupid in people.

He had no intention of acting as their nursemaid, Clementine Tyler or no. Whatever calamities befell them were on their shoulders, not his.

Then there was the war party. Once the Blackfeet became aware that a lot of whites had entered the range, they might take it into their heads to count as many coup as they could.

Fargo rubbed his chin and raised his head. He'd been so deep in thought, he hadn't been paying much attention to his surroundings. Now he focused on the next hill he had to cross before he reached the mountains and caught a flash of sunlight similar to the one he'd spotted back in town the day before.

Instantly, Fargo reined to the left. The whizz of lead preceded the far-off boom of the shot by a full second and a half.

Bending low over the saddle horn, Fargo used his spurs.

He'd almost forgotten about the Hollisters, but they sure as hell hadn't forgotten about him. Rance and that Sharps of his were becoming more than a nuisance.

Fargo flew into some pines. He drew rein, half expecting Rance to fire into the trees to try to pick him off. But Rance didn't waste the lead.

After waiting a while, Fargo continued on into the mountains, using every scrap of cover there was. The thickest trees, bluffs and rises he could keep between him and higher up—those sorts of things.

By early afternoon the foothills were behind and below him.

Twisting in the saddle, Fargo saw the ranch buildings in the distance and the spread of prairie to the east.

He went on climbing.

There was plenty of animal sign. Deer were numerous, and he saw a few elk. Smaller game were everywhere.

It was the middle of the afternoon when he stopped at a stream to let the Ovaro drink and knelt to take a sip himself.

Not inches away was the day-old track of a bear. By its size and the pads and the claws, he knew it was a black bear print and not a griz. Black bears were usually harmless. They'd run at the sight of a man on horseback where a griz might decide it was hungry.

For half a mile or so he had a feathered companion. A jay flew from tree to tree and squawked at him as if it shared the Blackfoot dislike for white invaders. Finally it wearied of insulting him and winged off.

At one point a squirrel set up a considerable racket.

If the Blackfeet heard it, they'd likely investigate. But they didn't appear.

Shortly after, he came on horse tracks.

The horse was shod so the rider must be white. One of the bull hunters, Fargo reckoned. The prints were larger than most, and he recollected that the farmer, Humphries, had been riding an oversized plow horse.

Fargo hadn't gone fifty more yards when cap rock spread before him.

And there, at its edge, lay a body.

16

Fargo drew rein.

The bib overalls confirmed his hunch. There was no sign of the plow horse.

Palming his Colt, Fargo dismounted. He warily advanced until he was behind a tree near the dead farmer.

Humphries was sprawled belly-down, his head twisted to one side, his eyes wide open. He didn't wear a pistol but he'd had a rifle in a scabbard on the plow horse. Evidently, he'd been killed before he could grab it.

Fargo eased from concealment. When nothing happened, he hunkered and rolled the body over. He had to use both hands, the man was so heavy.

The cause of death was obvious: a knife wound to the heart.

Since Humphries would never let the Blackfeet get that close— and he still had his hair—it ruled out the war party. Whoever stuck the knife in him had been white. Someone Humphries let come right up to him. Someone he wouldn't have suspected.

Based on how warm the body was, Fargo guessed that the farmer hadn't been dead half an hour, if that. The killer couldn't have gone far.

He straightened and saw two people standing and staring down at him from a little higher up and off to the right. They had the reins to their mounts in their hands, and when he set eyes on them, the woman gave a friendly wave.

Glyn and Aramone Richmond led their horses down. Glyn also held a lead rope to their pack animal. Both acted surprised when they saw Humphries.

"What's this?" Glyn said.

"We stopped to rest and saw you come out of the trees," Aramone said.

"You didn't notice the body?" Fargo asked.

"From up where we were you can't see it," Glyn said, and his eyes narrowed in suspicion. "Did you kill him?"

"Why the hell would I?"

"How would I know?" Glyn said. "I don't know a thing about you. Or him, for that matter."

"That works both ways," Fargo said.

"Please, let's not jump to conclusions," Aramone interjected, glancing at her brother. "It could have been anyone who killed this poor man."

Even you, Fargo thought, but he kept that to himself.

"Well, this is just dandy," Glyn said. "We must have a murderer among us."

"We should bury him," Aramone said.

"Without a shovel or a pick?" Glyn responded. "We'd waste an hour or more, as hard as the ground is."

"It's wrong to just leave him there like that," Aramone said.

"How so? We don't know him. We don't owe him anything."

Aramone appealed to Fargo. "What do you say we should do?"

Fargo agreed with her brother but for a different reason. "Whoever killed him might still be around. And there's the Blackfeet to think of."

"So you're saying we leave him there to rot?"

"He'll rot underground, too."

"Yes, but . . ." Aramone looked at her brother and at Fargo. "All right. I'm against it but if that's what you want, that's what we'll do."

Fargo wondered if it was an act on her part. What did she care about a complete stranger?

They climbed on their horses while he went for the Ovaro. Together, they scaled the cap rock to the next timber.

Fargo made it a point to let them go first. He'd rather have them in front of him than at his back. He couldn't think of a reason for them to kill the farmer, but he'd be damned if he'd trust them.

"We should make camp and talk this over," Aramone proposed.

"And waste hours of daylight?" Glyn said, shaking his head. "What purpose would it serve? I say we keep searching for the bull."

Once again Fargo agreed.

Aramone slowed so her sorrel could pace the Ovaro. "I'm sorry about my brother," she said. "He's not exactly a fount of human kindness."

"Who is?" Fargo said.

"He's always been more practical than me," Aramone remarked. "I suppose I should be grateful."

"Neither of you should be here."

"That's a fine thing to say. Especially since I think it's wonderful, us joining up."

"Oh?"

"When we make camp, we'll have the whole night ahead of us." Aramone grinned. "Whatever will we do with ourselves?"

"You have something in mind?"

Her gaze drifted to a spot several inches below his belt buckle. "As a matter of fact, I do."

17

Supper consisted of stew and biscuits.

Glyn cooked, not Aramone. They had enough grub on their packhorse to last a month of Sundays. None of it beans, Fargo's staple. They'd brought flour and sugar and a sack of potatoes and carrots, of all things. Fargo hardly ever saw anyone pack carrots.

The meat in the stew was rabbit.

Glyn shot it, not Fargo. It had broken from cover ahead of them and stopped, as rabbits often did, to look back and see if they were giving chase. And just like that, Glyn's hand whipped under his jacket and reappeared holding a Colt pocket pistol and he put a slug in the rabbit's head.

It was some shooting, Fargo had to admit. It raised his estimation of Richmond and also provoked a few questions.

Now, seated across from them as they dipped their spoons in their bowls and hungrily ate, Fargo voiced one of them.

"Where'd you learn to shoot like that?"

Glyn paused with his spoon half raised. "I've hunted a lot."

"Most hunters back east use a rifle."

"Depends on what you hunt," Glyn said, and Aramone laughed.

They seemed to be expecting him to ask, so Fargo did. "What did you hunt?"

"Men, and a few females besides."

"You're a bounty hunter?" Fargo asked in surprise.

"We both are."

Aramone piped up with, "They offer bounties east of the Mississippi River the same as they do west of it. Outlaws, debt shirks, escaped slaves, you name it."

"And you help him?"

"She does more than help," Glyn said. "We're in this as equals."

"You're a long way from the States," Fargo said.

"A bounty brought us here," Aramone said. "A man wanted in Missouri for a killing. We took up his trail and he crossed the Mississippi to get away from us."

"We caught up with him near Fort Laramie," Glyn took up the account. "That's where we saw a circular about the bull."

"And five thousand dollars is five thousand dollars," Aramone said.

"So here we are," Glyn said.

"That money is as good as ours," Aramone boasted.

Not in a million years would Fargo have taken them for bounty hunters. He digested the revelation as he ate.

Glyn didn't talk much but Aramone sure loved to.

Now that they'd revealed their secret, she had more to say about it.

"You seem surprised to hear what we do. I suppose it must seem strange for a woman to be in the bounty business, but my brother and I have always done everything together. When we were little, we spent all our time in the woods hunting and fishing. Our father never liked that I dressed as a boy and carried a rifle around."

"He ran an export business," Glyn mentioned.

"We had a fine house and fine clothes but I'd always dress scruffy and go off into the Pine Barrens to hunt."

"Pine Barrens?" Fargo said.

"In New Jersey," Aramone said.

"New Jersey bounty hunters," Fargo marveled. "Now I've heard everything."

Aramone laughed. "It's an uncommon profession for someone from New Jersey, I'll admit."

"I wouldn't do anything else," Glyn said. "Hunting for bounty suits me down to my marrow."

Fargo wondered what Rafer Crown would think of the news.

Aramone gazed at the sparkling stars and then out over the darkling silhouettes of high peaks. "I sure do like these mountains of yours."

"The Rockies aren't New Jersey," Fargo said.

"They're covered with woods and we know woods," Aramone said. "Don't worry about us. We're right at home here."

Fargo doubted it. "Say that again after you've run into a grizzly or the Blackfeet."

49

"Indians don't scare us," Glyn said. "I can shoot them as quick as I shot that rabbit."

"Rabbits don't shoot back," Fargo said. "And rabbits don't slit your throat while you're sleeping so they can lift your scalp and steal your horse."

"We're perfectly capable of defending ourselves," Aramone insisted.

"You'd better hope so," Fargo said.

18

The meal was done and the fire was being allowed to burn low.

Fargo lay on his back with his saddle for a pillow and an arm behind his head.

The Richmonds had spread their blankets and Glyn was on his side, his back to the fire.

Aramone lay facing the flames and Fargo. She'd closed her eyes a while ago and Fargo figured she was in dreamland until he saw her staring at him over her blanket. She raised her head and glanced at her brother as if to make sure he couldn't see her. Then, grinning at Fargo, she slowly rimmed her lips with the tip of her tongue and settled down as if to sleep.

Gradually, the flames dwindled to fingers.

Fatigue nipped at Fargo. He felt himself dozing off and tried to fight it but the next he knew, he was being shaken from a sound sleep by a hand on his shoulder. He opened his eyes.

Aramone was bent over him. Before she and her brother had turned in, she'd gone into the woods and changed from her riding outfit into a nightgown and heavy robe, which she now wore belted at the waist.

Putting a finger to her lips, she gestured at her brother, gripped Fargo's hand, and pulled.

Rising quietly, Fargo let her take him out of the circle of firelight into the trees. She went about twenty yards and faced him.

"This should be far enough," she whispered.

"Have something in mind, do you?" Fargo teased.

"I've been thinking of it all day," Aramone said throatily. "Hell, since I first set eyes on you."

Fargo still wasn't quite fully awake. He shook his head to clear it, and in the next moment she brazenly placed her hand between his legs.

"Look at what we have here," Aramone said. "Is this all it does, is hang there?"

Fargo woke up, right quick. The feel of her fingers caused him to swell and harden and a constriction to form in his throat. "You're asking for it."

"I wish to tell you I am." Aramone grinned and molded her mouth to his.

Fargo had been kissed by a lot of women in his time. Few were as talented. Aramone had a way of moving her lips and entwining her tongue that made it seem as if she were eating him alive. Their first kiss lasted a long while. When they finally parted, she was breathing heavily and her eyelids were hooded.

"Nice," she said.

Fargo cupped a breast and she cupped him again, down low.

"Oh my. How peculiar."

"What is?"

"You ride a stallion and you carry one around in your pants, too."

Chuckling, Fargo squeezed her tit, eliciting a moan and a flutter of her eyes.

"You sure know how to stoke a gal's fire."

"Do you know how to shut the hell up?" Fargo made sure she did by kissing her and digging his fingers into her bottom. She cooed and wriggled enticingly.

Prying at the cotton belt, Fargo parted her robe. Her nightgown was so sheer that her nipples jutted like twin tacks. He pinched one and then the other and she bit his shoulder and nipped his earlobe.

Fargo figured to ease her to the ground, but when he tried, she resisted and stood firm. He found out why when she undid his gun belt and his pants and delved a hand down in. At the contact, he involuntarily gasped.

"Like this, do you?"

Fargo liked it a lot. She commenced pushing his pants, and he helped. When they were down around his knees, she hiked at her nightgown and got it up around her waist.

"Guess what happens next."

"I gag you," Fargo said.

Aramone giggled, then placed her hands on his shoulders and wrapped her legs around his waist.

Fargo didn't know how she did it so quickly, but suddenly he was in her wet sheath. She arched her back and those luscious lips of her parted, and she slid down on him until he was all the way in.

"God, you feel good," she breathed.

Fargo couldn't speak for the constriction in his throat.

"You fill me like no man ever has," Aramone whispered.

Gripping her hips, Fargo began to slowly pump his legs.

"Yes," Aramone said. "Oh, yes."

They were both so enrapt in their pleasure that Fargo was slow to become aware of the stealthy crackle of the nearby undergrowth.

Something, or someone, was coming toward them.

19

Aramone heard it, too, and froze. "Do you hear that?" she whispered.

"Stay still," Fargo said. He glanced at the ground, and his gun belt. If he pulled out of her, he could drop to his knees and grab it.

"Do you think it's the Blackfeet?"

No, Fargo didn't. Most warriors had more sense than to go wandering around the mountains at night. Unless the war party had spotted the fire. He'd kept it small to prevent that, but you never knew.

"Maybe it's a bear."

Fargo doubted that, too. Normally, bears blundered about making more noise than the thing in the undergrowth. When stalking prey, though, they could be as silent as a cougar.

"Say something."

Fargo was about to slide out when the thing became visible. Only an inky outline but the shape was unmistakable.

"Why, it's just a doe," Aramone said. "Shoo!" she said, and waved a hand. "Leave us be!"

Spooked, the doe wheeled and bolted. The noise of her passage quickly faded and the woods were quiet again.

"Now where were we?" Aramone asked, her teeth a slash of white in the darkness.

Fargo was still rock hard. He resumed pumping with increased vigor until he was ramming up into her fit to cleave her in half.

"Yesssss," Aramone moaned. "Oh, yesssssss."

Fargo kissed and licked and caressed, and it wasn't long before she gasped and dug her nails into his shoulders and shuddered in ecstasy.

Presently Aramone sagged against him, saying softly in his ear, "That was nice."

"We're not done yet," Fargo said, and rammed into her anew.

"Oh God."

Fargo was in a mood to do it rough. He pinched her nipples until it had to hurt. He bit her neck. He squeezed her bottom so hard it would be a wonder if he didn't leave bruises.

Throwing back her head, Aramone closed her eyes and husked, "Don't stop. Don't ever stop."

Fargo didn't have a say in the matter. His body had taken over. Swept up in a rising tide of sensual pleasure, he let himself go. The explosion about curled his toes.

When at last he stopped, he received a grateful wet kiss on his cheek.

"Thank you, handsome."

Fargo grunted.

"I'd like to do that again real soon," she said dreamily.

"We'll see." Fargo still didn't completely trust her or her brother. Their denials that they hadn't killed Humphries didn't hold water, although he had to admit he couldn't think of a reason why they would.

Aramone was playing with his hair. "I love it," she said. "I love it more than anything. My brother says it's not proper, that a true lady would never admit such a thing. But what am I to do? Lie?"

Fargo would be the first to admit that it was harder for a woman to admit to liking carnal relations, as they were called, than it was for a man. Women who did were usually branded whores.

"He says I'll never find a husband if I give it away for free," Aramone had gone on and lightly laughed. "He doesn't realize I like giving it away."

"Put yourself together," Fargo said. He did the same, glad to have the Colt around his waist again. He loosened it in his holster as he followed her back.

Glyn Richmond was still on his side, breathing evenly in the rhythm of deep sleep.

Aramone grinned as she sank down. Pulling her blanket to her neck, she blew him a kiss. "'Night," she whispered.

Fargo figured sleep would come quickly but he lay there a good half an hour before his eyelids grew leaden.

He slept uneasily. Twice he awakened. Once when a wolf howled and one of their horses nervously whinnied. The second time, he heard the Richmonds whispering to each other. He couldn't catch the words but they appeared to be having an argument. He made the mistake of rolling toward them to hear better, and they immediately stopped.

Daybreak broke crisp and cool. Fargo was up first and rekindled the fire. He put coffee on and the aroma brought Aramone up onto her elbows.

"Morning," she said with another of her inviting smiles. "I slept like a baby last night. How about you?"

"Not so much," Fargo said.

She gazed at the spreading rosy glow to the east. "It promises to be a gorgeous day."

At that moment, from off up the mountain, came the crack of a shot.

20

Glyn Richmond sat up. He was fully awake and must have been for some time. Cocking his head, he said, "That wasn't more than half a mile off."

Fargo was impressed. It took a good ear to tell that.

"Could be someone shooting game for breakfast," Aramone speculated.

"A dumb thing to do with the Blackfeet in the area," Glyn said.

Fargo thought that a dumb thing to say, given that Richmond had shot a rabbit the day before.

"If the Blackfeet go after them and not us, I say let them be as careless as they want to be," Aramone said and laughed.

None of the bull hunters meant anything to Fargo, except for Crown and Peters. They'd sided with him against the Hollisters in the saloon, and he reckoned he owed them for that.

"Let's eat and get cracking," Glyn said. "We have a lot of riding to do."

"It will be wonderful to have your company," Aramone said to Fargo. "My brother isn't much of a conversationalist, I'm afraid."

Neither was Fargo. "We'll be parting ways."

"What?" Aramone looked hurt. "We should stick together for our mutual protection."

"I don't need protecting," Fargo said. And he could cover more ground alone.

"I must say I'm surprised at your attitude," Aramone said.

"I'm not," Glyn said. "It's the money. He doesn't want us with him if we come on the bull because he doesn't care to share it."

"Is that how it is?" Aramone asked. "You're just as greedy as everyone else?"

"Think what you want," Fargo said.

"I think I'd like some eggs," Glyn said.

They'd brought some, pressed into the flour so the shells would be less likely to break. Aramone plucked them out and her brother broke them over a frying pan. They also had bacon.

"Care for some?" Aramone asked Fargo. "To show there are no hard feelings?"

"Why would there be?" Fargo rejoined. He had to admit, the aroma of the sizzling bacon made his mouth water and his stomach rumble.

He almost changed his mind about going his own way. With food like that, and Aramone to treat himself to at night, he was giving up some prime pleasures. But as soon as they were saddled, he reined to the northwest, saying, "Keep your eyes skinned."

"Be careful, handsome," Aramone called after him.

"Enough with him," Glyn said, sounding annoyed. "We have a bull to find."

So did Fargo. The sooner he picked up Thunderhead's trail, the sooner he could claim the five thousand and be shed of the whole mess.

The trappers had seen Thunderhead about ten miles from the Tyler ranch. Fargo reckoned he had two or three miles to go yet before he would be in the vicinity.

To the east the sun blazed the sky as overhead a few cumulus clouds drifted. Sparrows flitted in the brush, a squirrel scampered in the high branches and several deer watched him from a distance.

Fargo breathed deep and smiled. He'd take this any day over the bustle and stink of a town. Then again, up here he couldn't sit in on a game of poker or bed a dove or wet his throat with whiskey unless he brought a bottle.

He was thinking that his ideal place would be a town far up in the mountains where he could enjoy the best of both worlds when movement snapped his gaze to a two-legged figure a quarter-mile higher.

Whoever it was, they were shambling along as if they were drunk. They weaved. They staggered. They were in the shadow of timber and he couldn't make out much until they stumbled into the open.

Fargo gave a start.

The figure wore a dress.

A jab of his spurs brought the stallion to a trot. He climbed half the distance before he recognized who it was, and then he rode faster.

She was barely able to stay on her feet. Stumbling, she almost fell. The heavy Colt Dragoon in her hand didn't help her balance any.

She didn't seem to notice him, not even when he drew rein not ten feet from her.

"Esther?" Fargo said.

The old woman's eyes were half shut and she had blood smeared over most of her face. She had been shot in the head, just below the hairline. A crease, it looked like, and it had bled fierce.

"Esther?" Fargo said again, alighting.

Esther blinked and jerked her head up. "Who's there?" she demanded, weakly raising the Dragoon in both hands.

"Skye Fargo. You met me at the Tyler's, remember?"

Esther pointed her hand-cannon in his direction. "Was it you who shot me?"

"Sure wasn't," Fargo said.

"I don't believe you," Esther said and cocked the Dragoon.

21

Her Colt Dragoon was an older model. Fargo could tell by the cylinder notches and the trigger guard. A .44-caliber, it packed a considerable wallop.

"It wasn't me," Fargo said. "If I wanted you dead, I'd have finished you off instead of riding up to see if you were all right."

Esther swayed and steadied herself and shook her head. "I don't know. I suppose you would at that. God, it hurts." She blinked furiously, and only then did Fargo realize she couldn't see for all the blood in her eyes.

"Esther, you need to let me help you."

"I'd just gotten up," she said. "The shot came out of nowhere." She slowly lowered the Colt and eased down the hammer. "Hell," she said and collapsed.

In a bound Fargo caught her. As small and frail-seeming as she was, she weighed no more than a feather. Scooping her into his arms, he held on to the Ovaro's reins and retraced her steps up the mountain.

She had made camp in a small clearing. Her fire still crackled, and her horse and pack animal were still picketed. Splatters of blood near the fire showed where she had been when she was shot.

Fargo eased her down. The wound wasn't severe enough to be fatal unless it became infected. She had a water bag and he filled her coffeepot and put the water on to boil.

In her pack he found a towel, which he cut into strips with the Arkansas toothpick.

The whole time he worked, Fargo kept one eye on the surrounding timber. Whoever tried to splatter her brains might be lurking out there.

Once the water was warm, Fargo washed the blood from her

face and cleaned the wound. He wrapped a strip around her head and was tying it when her eyes fluttered open and she looked dazedly about.

"It's all right," Fargo said. "You're safe."

Alertness returned, and Esther reached up and touched the bandage. "Like hell. But I thank you." She went to sit up and he pressed on her shoulder to keep her down.

"Rest a while yet. You're still woozy."

"Damned scalawag," Esther muttered.

"Is that your notion of thanks?"

"Not you," Esther said. "The son of a bitch who shot me."

"Either he's a poor shot or you turned your head as he squeezed the trigger," Fargo said.

"The shot came from yonder," Esther said, pointing to the west. "It knocked me flat and I was bleeding something awful. I crawled into the trees and don't remember much after that."

"I found you wandering."

"No sign of anyone else?"

Fargo told her about finding Humphries and meeting up with the Richmonds. "They're the only ones I've seen besides you."

"It couldn't have been one of them who shot me, then, since they were with you." Esther winced and closed her eyes. "You know what this means, don't you? First that farmer, now me."

Fargo had already realized the obvious. "Someone is out to kill the bull hunters."

"The bastard wants to be sure he collects the bounty."

"You sure have a mouth on you." Fargo tried to make light of the situation.

"I've had my head creased with lead and it hurts like hell," Esther rejoined. "Excuse me for being a grump, you silly jackass."

Fargo laughed. "Is there anything I can get you?"

"Some coffee would be nice. I was about to put some on when I was shot."

Fargo busied himself, again with an eye to the forest. He also watched the Ovaro. The stallion would warn him if it caught the scent of anyone skulking about or heard something.

"This is a fine how-do-you-do," Esther said bitterly. "There were several other women besides me, and those three redheaded sprouts with their squirrel rifles."

Fargo had forgotten about the kids.

"Whoever it is who shot me is a miserable coward," Esther said. "Shooting an old gal like me from ambush."

"He was probably scared of your Dragoon."

"Mind your elders, buckskin," Esther said. "And he should be scared. I find out who did this, I will put a bullet between their eyes."

"You should head back down once you're up to it," Fargo advised.

"What in hell for?"

"You've been shot."

"No one knows that better than me, you lunkhead. But I repeat: What in hell for?"

"So you won't be shot again."

"Just because I have wrinkles doesn't make me stupid. From here on out I don't put myself in a position to be shot."

Fargo thought of the two tries on his life by Rance Hollister. "You never know."

"Hell, that can be said about anything in life. I have never been timid and I won't start now."

"If you get yourself killed, don't expect me to shed any tears."

"A smart-mouth like you?" Esther retorted. "Besides, we hardly know each other. All you know about me is that I'm old and grumpy—"

"And had a husband named Charlie."

"—and all I know about you is that you're damned good-looking and you make cow eyes at every pretty filly you see."

"I do not."

Esther snorted. "I saw you with that gal with the parasol down to Tyler's. You damn near drooled over her."

"You need your eyes checked, old woman."

"And you need to keep yours in the back of your head, young man. Because as sure as shooting, whoever killed poor Humphries and tried to do the same to me will get around to putting lead into you."

22

Fargo stayed with Esther another hour. He was willing to stay longer. He liked the feisty gray-haired hen. But she shooed him off, saying she didn't want him sitting there staring at her. She'd recovered enough that he knew she could manage.

Once in the saddle, Fargo searched the forest to the west. He was looking for some sign of the shooter. He spent another hour at it and found no tracks, no trace, nothing.

He headed northwest again, on the lookout for a sign of Thunderhead. He couldn't imagine what had brought the bull up into the high country other than the contrary natures bulls were noted for.

A switchback brought him to a tableland rich with grass sprinkled by islands of trees. The bull would have plenty of graze but he found no evidence it had been there.

A glimmer of blue drew him to a spring at the far end. Cottonwoods shimmered in the sunlight and a dragonfly flitted about.

Dismounting, he let the Ovaro drink. A handy log looked inviting. No sooner did he sit, though, than who should come traipsing out of the cottonwoods but the three redheaded boys. Each held a squirrel rifle but made no attempt to bring it to bear. Their homespun clothes showed a lot of wear. Their pants had holes in them. Their shoes looked ready to fall apart. Their faces were grimy with dirt and their hair was cut so unevenly and poorly, it was obvious they did the cutting themselves.

"Howdy, mister," said the first and tallest.

"What do we have here?" Fargo said.

"You have the Johnsons," the tallest boy said. "I'm Solomon but mostly I answer to Sol. My middle brother here is Seth. And the youngest is Jared."

"Where are your folks?" Fargo asked.

"Dead," Sol answered. "Some four years now."

"We make do on our own," Seth declared.

"Yep," Jared said.

They set the stocks of their squirrel rifles on the ground and leaned on the barrels. All three had blue eyes and pug noses and oval chins. All three looked about as formidable as chipmunks.

"You shouldn't be here," Fargo said.

"We have the same right to go after the bull as anybody," Sol said.

"This is no place for amateurs."

"We're pint-sized but we have bark on us," Seth said. "Anyone gives us trouble, we'll learn them not to."

"We will," Jared said.

Fargo had met his share of kids set adrift. Life on the frontier was hard. Some would say it was merciless. Fathers were thrown from horses and broke their necks or were dashed to death from moving wagons or took deathly sick or were caught by hostiles. Mothers didn't seem to suffer as many accidents but once they lost their man, their futures were bleak. Work was hard to come by, especially work that paid enough for a mother to feed and clothe herself and her children, to say nothing of keeping a roof over their heads. A lot of widows drowned their sorrows in alcohol and drowned themselves in the bargain.

"You don't have any uncles or aunts?"

"We're fine on our own," Sol said.

"That we are," Seth echoed.

"We don't need anybody," little Jared said.

"Do you have horses?" Fargo asked.

"We'd be plumb stupid to be up here without any," Sol said and bobbed his head at the cottonwoods. "They're hid so the redskins won't spot us."

"Smart," Fargo said.

"Tell us about you, mister," Seth said. "We heard tell you scout for the army."

"Sometimes."

"We heard you track real good, too," little Jared said.

Sol nodded. "We talked to Mr. Tyler and he said that you and the jasper who wears two pistols and that other fella with the moccasins are the three best trackers of the bunch."

"We probably are," Fargo allowed.

"Then you three have the best chance of any of us of findin' that bull."

"It will be luck as much as anything."

"We believe in makin' our own luck," Sol said. "And we want that five thousand."

"We'd be rich," Seth said.

"Rich," Jared echoed.

Fargo frowned. Trying to talk them out of it was pointless. His only recourse was to take their rifles and make them mount up and escort them back down the mountain. The only thing was, there was no one to look after them, and the moment he headed back up, so would they.

"Why do you look so glum, mister?" Sol asked.

First it was the old hen and now these infants. "It's been a hell of a day," Fargo said.

Jared squinted at the sun and remarked, "Heck, mister. It's not half over."

"Don't remind me," Fargo said.

23

The Ovaro was done drinking and Fargo didn't have a lot of time to spare. Standing, he came right out with, "Is there any chance I can talk you out of hunting for the bull?"

"Not a snowball's," Sol said.

"We have it to do," Seth said.

Jared nodded.

"You could get killed," Fargo bluntly brought up.

"Not likely," Sol said.

"We're too clever," Seth said.

"Like foxes," from Jared.

"You have a high opinion of yourselves," Fargo mentioned.

"You did hear me say our folks have been dead goin' on four years?" Sol said.

"How do you reckon we've lasted so long?" Seth asked.

"We're foxes," little Jared said.

"Damn it, boys," Fargo said.

They looked at one another and Jared cradled his squirrel rifle and said, "We savvy that you're worried about us, mister. That's nice, you bein' a stranger, and all. People do it all the time. Because we're kids, they figure we need lookin' after."

"But we don't," Seth said.

"We surely don't," Jared declared.

"There are Blackfeet . . ." Fargo began.

"Injuns don't scare us none," Sol said. "We've kilt a few when we've had to."

"We'll kill more if need be," Seth said.

"I like killin'," Jared declared.

Fargo had done all he could. Before he rode off, he warned them that, "There's something else. Someone has killed one of the bull hunters and tried to kill another."

"By someone you don't mean the redskins?" Sol asked.

"I mean white."

They looked at one another again and Sol said, "You say only one has been kilt?"

"The farmer. His name was Humphries."

"Met him," Sol said.

"Not too bright," Seth said.

"Nope," Jared said.

"The old woman was shot but she'll live," Fargo let them know.

"You don't say," Sol said and looked at Jared.

"I wish you would reconsider staying in the hunt."

"Five thousand is more than we could make any way except stealin' it," Sol said. "We can't pass this up."

Both Seth and Jared shook their heads and Jared said, "Can't."

"Suit yourselves." Fargo stepped to the Ovaro, gripped the saddle horn, and swung up. As he settled himself, the three came over.

"We like you, mister," Sol said. "We think you'll likely be the one."

"Yep," Seth said.

For once Jared didn't contribute.

"Good luck," Sol said. "Watch out for the redskins and those Hollisters we heard about who are after you and anything else that might want to do you in."

"You need to find the bull," Seth said.

"Find it," Jared said.

Fargo gigged the Ovaro. He glanced back after he had gone a short way but the boys weren't there. They had disappeared into the cottonwoods. "That was damn strange," he summed it up, and put them from his mind.

He needed to stay sharp as a razor. The woods were crawling with enemies. Not literally, but there were enough that all it would take was for him to let down his guard for a moment and he'd wind up like Humphries.

He thought he might come on more of the bull hunters since they were all headed in the same general direction, but the afternoon waxed and waned and he saw no one else.

Toward sundown he came on a ribbon of a stream and made camp. He didn't bother with a fire. It would serve as a beacon to those inclined to do him in. A cold camp sufficed. He drank mountain water and chewed pemmican from his saddlebag.

It had been an eventful day. He lay reviewing all that had happened until sleep claimed him. His rest, once again, was fitful. He woke up at the slightest or farthest of sounds and then would lie there a while before he could get back to sleep.

Toward dawn he awoke feeling as if he hadn't slept a wink. Throwing his blanket off, he got up, decided to hell with it, and put coffee on. When it was hot, he downed three cups and almost felt like himself.

He was tightening the cinch on his saddle, about to head out, when a shot crackled and echoed. This time it came from lower down. Not more than a quarter-mile, he reckoned, and as he scoured the slopes he had climbed the day before, he spied the red and orange of dancing flames.

It was stupid to go back, he chided himself. He should press on after the bull. But he reined down the mountain, not up, and in half an hour came to a halt in a clearing.

"Hell," Fargo said.

Esther was flat on her back with her arms outflung and a look of surprise on her wrinkled face. The Dragoon was in its holster. She still wore the bandage. Only now, an inch below it was a new bullet hole. Someone had shot her in the center of her forehead as she was making coffee of her own.

"You should have listened, old woman," Fargo said.

He had a choice. Leave her for the buzzards and other scavengers or bury her. The smart thing was to leave her.

Fargo climbed down. With a fallen tree limb that had a jagged tip, he dug a shallow grave. She had nothing on her, no purse, no poke, nothing. He didn't say any words over the grave. What was the point?

Her mule and packhorse hadn't been taken. More proof it wasn't the Blackfeet. He rigged a lead rope and slipped it over each.

They would slow him down. But his only recourse was to point them down the mountain and smack them on the rump, and they might die untended.

By noon he was close to where the trappers must have seen Thunderhead. He scoured for sign, and it wasn't ten minutes later that he sat staring down at week-old tracks.

"God in heaven," he breathed.

They were huge. The largest hoofprints he'd ever come across. Thunderhead wasn't just a bull. He was a monster.

When Fargo squatted and held his hand to one of the tracks, his fingers weren't long enough to reach the other side.

Straightening, he scanned the timber above. He didn't spot the bull.

But he did see the Blackfeet.

24

There were seven. They were descending an open slope in single file. Even at that distance, Fargo saw their war paint.

Quickly, Fargo pulled the Ovaro and the mule and the packhorse into cover. He prayed the Blackfeet hadn't caught sight of him. He would rather avoid them than fight. This was their land, not his. He was just another invader.

When the mule and the packhorse were swallowed by forest, he climbed on the Ovaro and rode due north. His aim was to swing wide of the war party. But he hadn't gone half a mile when he looked back and there they were.

They'd seen him, all right.

And they were after him.

"Hell," Fargo growled.

Since he couldn't outrun them leading the extras, he reluctantly let go of the lead rope and used his spurs. He needn't worry that the mule and the packhorse would be eaten. The Blackfeet weren't like the Apaches, to whom a roasted horse, or mule, was delicious.

Too, Fargo figured the war party would stop to claim their prizes, buying him time to increase his lead. But the Blackfeet left only one warrior to handle them and the rest came on at a gallop.

Fargo was careful not to push the Ovaro too hard. Its stamina was second to none, and if he did this smart, he could outlast them.

The thought of "smart" make him think of the three freckled kids. They were lucky the Blackfeet saw him and not them. Could be that the Blackfeet would take them prisoner, rather than kill them, and possibly adopt them into the tribe.

The next time Fargo looked back, he couldn't see the war party. He expected them to appear out of the trees but they didn't.

He stopped to give the Ovaro a brief breather, and that was when he spotted them again.

The wily warriors had split. Three had borne to the west and three to the east, and now they were coming on fast. Their intent was clear. To catch him between them.

Fargo pushed on to a broad ridge. Deadfall covered the next slope. Firs, hundreds of them, lay as if flattened by a tempest. He skirted them and came to the top and stopped.

He needed to discourage the war party and this was as good a spot as any. Shucking the Henry from his saddle scabbard, he roosted on a convenient stump.

It wasn't long before the warriors to the east broke into the open, followed shortly after by the warriors to the west. They signaled one another and met up at the bottom of the deadfall.

They weren't quite in range yet but Fargo brought the Henry to his shoulder. Two warriors appeared to be arguing over something. Maybe whether to keep on after him.

The argument ended and they moved to come around the tangle as he'd done.

Fargo sat motionless except for thumbing back the Henry's hammer. When he was sure, he held his breath to steady the rifle and stroked the trigger.

The lead warrior jerked at the impact and clutched his shoulder but wasn't unhorsed. The whole war party immediately turned and streaked to the bottom.

Fargo smiled. That should discourage them. Hopping off the stump, he shoved the Henry into the scabbard, forked leather, and rode like a bat out of Hades for pretty near half an hour. The next time he looked back, he'd lost them.

He was pleased with himself. He'd avoided killing them.

It bothered him, though, that they continued to pose a threat to the bull hunters. Anyone they counted coup on was on his shoulders.

Troubled, he commenced to circle back to where he had found Thunderhead's tracks. He'd covered about half the distance when the Ovaro snorted and shied, and glancing about, he discovered why.

Two bull hunters were over under a spruce. They had spread out their blankets the night before and turned in, and sometime during the night someone had slit their throats from ear to ear. Pools of blood had collected under and around them, and it was the stink that caused the Ovaro to react.

Fargo remembered seeing them at the ranch but he'd never learned their names. They were faces in the money-hungry crowd, nothing more.

Their horses were tied to the tree. Their rifles were by their sides. Plainly, the Blackfeet weren't to blame here, either.

Whoever killed Humphries and Esther had claimed two more.

Fargo sought some clue to the killer's identity. The carpet of needles under the spruce didn't bear prints. He ranged wider but all he found were a few scrapes.

Whoever the killer was, he was damn good.

Fargo wasn't about to bury these two. He did go through their pockets and their saddlebags and found it interesting that he didn't find any money. Not a single cent between them. He hadn't found any money on Esther, either.

Unfurling, he turned to the Ovaro to climb back on.

And froze when a gun hammer clicked behind him.

25

"Well, look at who we have here," said a familiar icy voice.

"Want me to shoot him, Rance?" Grizz Hollister asked.

"Hell no," Rance answered. "We're goin' to have some fun with him first."

"I like havin' fun," Kyler Hollister said.

Fargo wanted to kick himself. He'd been so caught up in the bodies, he hadn't kept an eye out.

"You can turn your head but only your head," Rance said.

Fargo did. Rance was pointing his Sharps, Grizz his revolver, and Kyler had his hand on the antler hilt to his long knife but hadn't slid it from its sheath. "Did you kill these two?" he asked the latter, nodding at the men with their throats slit.

"Weren't me," Kyler said. "Not that I wouldn't if I was of a mind."

"Maybe it was him," Grizz said, gesturing with his six-shooter at Fargo.

"No, not him," Rance said. "Not the famous scout. He doesn't back-shoot or kill folks in their sleep."

"We do," Kyler said and laughed.

Rance took a step, his finger curled around the Sharps's trigger. "Here's how it will be. You do exactly as I say or I blow a hole in you as big as my fist."

Fargo boiled with anger.

"First, take your hand off that saddle horn and hold both your arms out where I can see your hands. No tricks, or I squeeze."

Fargo complied.

"Good. Now, two fingers and two fingers only, pluck that smoke wagon and toss it. Nice and slow or I squeeze."

"I'll squeeze too," Grizz said.

Every fiber of his being screamed at him not to but Fargo relieved himself of the Colt.

"There," Rance said smugly. "I've trimmed your claw."

"You're forgettin' something," Kyler said. "What I told you about."

"Oh. That's right." Rance stared at Fargo's boot. "My brother says you carry a hideout pigsticker. Two fingers, ease it out and add it to the pile."

As slow as molasses, once again Fargo did as he was told.

Rance smirked and took another step and kicked the Colt and the Arkansas toothpick away. "There. Now we are safe."

"He's not," Kyler said.

"I want first crack," Grizz said. "He hurt me back in town. I owe him."

"We all owe him," Rance said. "We'll do this my way. You'll have your turn when I say."

Fargo was curious. "How did you find me?"

"We've been huntin' that bull, the same as everybody," Rance said, "and caught sight of you ridin' like hell from a pack of red-skins. Wasn't no feat for us to trail you. You and the redskins only had eyes for each other."

"Damn me," Fargo said.

Kyler drew his foot-and-a-half-long knife. "Enough talk. How about I carve on him some? A couple fingers, a couple of toes. Or let me cut off his nose and ears."

"You'll cut when I say you can cut," Rance said.

Kyler didn't like that. "You're awful bossy today."

"Who's the oldest?" Rance said.

"But still," Kyler responded.

"Grizz, fetch our horses," Rance commanded, and when his hulking brother wheeled and lumbered off, Rance chuckled at Fargo and asked, "Scared yet?"

Fargo didn't reply.

"You will be," Rance vowed. He nudged his younger brother. "What are you standin' there for? There are two dead men for you to search."

"Oh," Kyler said, and stepped to the bodies.

"You won't find any money," Fargo said.

"Did you take it already?" Rance asked.

"There wasn't any."

"Whoever slit their throats robbed them, too?" Kyler said. "That's somethin' we would do."

Fargo gauged the distance between him and Rance and decided not to try. It would take at least two long bounds and Rance would easily put a slug into him. Figuring to distract Rance into lowering the Sharps, he asked, "Was it you who killed the old woman and the farmer?"

"We haven't killed anyone in a couple of months," Rance said.

"But we sure as hell will be killin' you," Kyler said.

"You're sayin' more have been kilt like these two?" Rance asked.

"The old woman was shot," Fargo said. "The farmer took a knife to the heart."

"And now these two with their throats cut," Rance said, and laughed. "Well, I'll be damned."

"What?" Kyler asked.

"Don't you see, little brother? Someone is goin' around snuffin' the wicks of all the bull hunters."

"How come?"

"You must not have a brain," Rance said. "Whoever it is, is killin' off the competition."

"Doesn't mean the killer will be the one to find the bull," Kyler pointed out the flaw in the plan.

"Could be he just wants to increase his chances," Rance guessed. He looked at Fargo. "Is that how you read it?"

"It's one way," Fargo said.

Hooves thudded, and off through the trees Grizz approached, leading their horses by the reins. He saw Rance and smiled and waved.

"Jackass," Rance said.

"He's just bein' friendly," Kyler said.

"He's still a jackass."

"I'd like to see you tell him that to his face."

"I said he's a jackass. Not me."

Fargo tensed to spring. Rance was looking at Grizz, not at him. But just as he was about to, Rance faced him and raised the Sharps.

"Now, then, let's tie his wrists and string him up and get to it."

26

It was hell not being able to do anything.

Fargo had to stand there with Rance covering him while Grizz tied one end of a rope around his ankles. Kyler was busy throwing the other end over a low limb on the spruce.

"Scared yet?" Rance taunted once more.

"The Blackfeet might still be hunting for me," Fargo mentioned.

"So? We see them, we'll light a shuck and leave you hangin' for them to play with."

"I'd as soon kill him," Grizz said. "Redskins do things even I wouldn't do." He had looped the rope twice and was about to tie a knot.

"Listen to you, weak sister," Rance said.

"Don't call me names," Grizz rumbled.

Fargo had to do something. In another moment the rope would be tight.

As if sensing that he was about to be reckless, Rance stepped in close and jammed the Sharps's muzzle against his chest. "Go ahead. Try somethin'. I welcome an excuse."

Kyler laughed. "Brother, you're a caution." He caught hold of the end of the rope dangling from the limb and pulled to take up the slack so there was enough for him to wrap it around the trunk. "We're about set for the carvin'."

"Grizz, you do the honors," Rance said. "You're strong as anything."

Fargo braced himself but it still hurt when Grizz yanked on the rope, sweeping his legs out from under him, and he crashed to earth. Grizz went on pulling, and in no time Fargo was hanging upside down, his hat on the ground under him.

Kyler, meanwhile, was securing the rope to the trunk. Several loops sufficed. When he had it tied off, he stepped back and said, "There."

Rance shouldered the Sharps and came up and punched Fargo in the gut.

Waves of pain about blacked Fargo out. He grit his teeth to keep from crying out as he turned first one way and then another.

Grizz laughed. "Hit him again."

"Hit, hell," Kyler said. "Use my knife."

"We take our time at this," Rance said. "Tough hombre like him should last a day or two."

"Days?" Kyler said. "We ain't never carved on anyone that long."

"He'll be the first."

Kyler drew his long-bladed knife, gripped Fargo by the hair to keep him still, and held the razor tip close to Fargo's right eye. "How about I take this out to start? They always scream when I do that."

"I want him to see the rest of it," Rance said.

"He'll still have one eye."

"Cut off his nose or an ear if you want but not the eyes yet."

"Hell, he won't scream over a nose or an ear," Kyler complained.

"Did I ask or did I tell you?"

Kyler swore and lowered his knife. "If that's the case, do what you want and when you're finished I'll start in on him."

"I get to hurt him, too," Grizz said. "He hurt me at the saloon."

"You can break all the bones you want," Rance said, "so long as it doesn't kill him until I'm good and ready."

Grizz's dull eyes lit with excitement. "I like to break bones. I like to hear them crack."

"We each have our pleasures," Rance said.

"A whore gives me pleasure," Kyler said. "Carvin' on a man is fun."

"I like to have fun with my whores," Grizz said. "I bounce them on my knees."

"Why are we talkin' about whores?" Rance asked.

"Kyler brought them up," Grizz said. "I was only sayin'."

Rance turned to Fargo. "About recovered from that punch, are you?" he asked and punched Fargo again in the same spot.

The pain was doubly worse. Fargo grimaced and struggled not to black out as he swung to the right and then the left.

"Aww, I bet that hurt," Kyler said, laughing.

"Maybe we can make him cry," Grizz said.

"Not this hombre," Rance said, giving Fargo's chest a thwack with the back of his hand. "He's as tough as they come."

"Even the tough ones break if you work on them long enough," Kyler said.

"You are young but you've learned," Rance complimented him. He set himself and balled his fists.

"Hold him, both of you."

Grizz seized Fargo's right arm and Kyler gripped his left.

"Get ready for more pain," Rance said.

Fargo bunched his stomach muscles and the first few blows didn't hurt as much as before, but he couldn't do it indefinitely. By the seventh or eighth blow, the agony was excruciating. Bitter bile dribbled up his gorge into his mouth.

Rance hit and hit, smirking in vicious delight.

Fargo didn't know how much more he could take when, unexpectedly, Rance stopped and stepped back.

"Your turn, brother," he said to Grizz. "Time to break some of his bones."

27

Fargo was in serious trouble. Rance's blows were bad enough. Grizz was strong enough to not just break bones but burst his organs, besides. He'd once seen a man who had been beaten so severely, the man's intestines ruptured.

Grizz grinned as he moved to where Rance had been standing and Rance grasped Fargo's arm. Grizz held up a fist the size of a ham to Fargo's nose. "See this? I can bust boards with this."

Fargo spat on a walnut-sized knuckle.

Grizz drew his fist back and looked at the spit. "That wasn't nice."

"Get to it," Rance snapped.

Nodding, Grizz cocked his arm. "How about I start with his ribs?"

"Fine. Just so you don't kill him."

"Here goes," Grizz said.

Just then three shots rang out, *crack-crack-crack*, and Grizz clutched at his shoulder and cried, "I'm hit!"

"Me too!" Kyler yelled, clasping his left forearm.

Rance had set down his Sharps to take hold of Fargo, but now he scooped it up and fired off into the trees. "I don't see anybody!"

"It must be the redskins!" Kyler bawled.

Two more shots sounded, and Fargo heard the buzz of lead.

"I'm hit again!" Grizz bellowed, pressing a hand to his thigh.

"Run!" Rance hollered.

And they did, racing to their horses and scrambling onto their saddles. Grizz nearly fell off but managed, and as more shots cracked, they wheeled and jabbed their heels and fled. Several more shots were fired after them as if for good measure.

Then the woods fell quiet.

Fargo waited with half-bated breath. He, too, figured it must be the Blackfeet, although why they had contented themselves with shooting when they could have snuck up and taken the Hollisters captive was a mystery.

Figures appeared, three of them, sauntering toward him with smiles on their freckled faces and their red hair dappled by sunlight.

"I'll be damned," Fargo said.

"Well, look at you," Solomon Johnson said. "Trussed up and helpless."

"Plumb pitiful," Seth said.

"Scouts ain't much, are they?" little Jared said.

"He got caught easy enough," Sol said.

"Plumb pitiful," Seth said a second time.

"And he never once caught on we were followin' him," Jared said.

"Plumb pitiful," Seth said a third time.

Fargo had recovered from his initial surprise and growled, "Are you done insulting me?"

"Be nice," Sol said. "We just saved your bacon."

"Can't let you die," Seth said.

"We think you're the one who will do it," Jared threw in.

"Cut me down," Fargo said. "My toothpick is on the ground there next to my Colt."

"Don't need it. We carry our own blades." Sol handed his squirrel rifle to Seth, slid his right hand up his left sleeve and drew out a double-edged dagger.

"I'll be damned," Fargo said. "You boys don't miss a trick."

"The way we live, we can't afford to," Sol said, stepping to the tree.

"What's that mean?"

Instead of answering, Sol pressed his dagger to the rope and slashed. That was all it took.

Fargo tensed his shoulders and shifted so they took the brunt and not his neck and head. He lay there a few moments, collecting himself, the pain in his gut still bad enough to make him want to double over.

"You takin' a nap?" Sol asked.

"Scouts sure are puny," Seth said.

"Sure are," Jared echoed.

"You're not nearly as funny as you think you are," Fargo said dryly.

"Who's bein' funny?" Sol said.

Fargo got to his feet. He picked up the Colt and shoved it into his holster and picked up the toothpick, hiked his pant leg, and replaced it in its ankle sheath.

"First those redskins and now this," Sol said. "You need to watch out for yourself better."

"We don't want anything to happen to you," Seth said.

"Find the bull and quit playin' around," little Jared said.

Fargo glared at him.

"What?"

Sol had turned and was staring at the bodies of the men with their throats slit. "Look at that," he said.

His brothers turned.

"They bled out nice," Seth said.

"Bet they didn't hurt much," Jared said.

"They're still dead," Seth said. He claimed his rifle from his brother and peered off into the forest. "We'd best light a shuck. Those three might take it into their heads to circle back."

"Always play it safe," Seth said.

"Always," Jared said.

They started to walk off and Sol said over his shoulder to Fargo, "Be seein' you."

"Wait," Fargo said.

"No."

"Why are you following me?"

"We already told you," Sol said.

"Find the damn bull," Seth said.

"If you don't, you are worthless," little Jared said.

"Damn it," Fargo said, but they paid him no heed and melted into the undergrowth and were gone. He was tempted to go after them but they might be right about the Hollisters circling back.

Fargo stared at the throat-slit bodies and then off in the direction the Hollisters had gone and then in the direction the three boys had vanished and scratched his chin in bewilderment. "What the hell?"

28

If the Johnson boys were shadowing him, they were good at it.

Fargo tried to catch them. Several times he reined behind a pine or a boulder and waited for them to appear but they never did. Once he dismounted atop a ridge and lay on his belly for half an hour studying his back trail, but nothing.

They were ghosts, those boys.

He saw neither hide nor hair of anyone else, either. Apparently the war party had lost his trail, and he could devote himself to finding Thunderhead's.

Toward sundown the terrain underwent a change. Canyons and bluffs replaced the steep slopes, and there were far fewer trees.

He stopped for the night in a gully deep enough to hide him and the Ovaro. After the day he'd had, he decided to treat himself, and his belly, to coffee. It took a while to gather enough wood and dry brush. He kept the fire small and, as the coffeepot heated, reviewed the day's events.

Something nagged at him, a vague sense that an important fact was right in front of his face but he was missing it.

The coffee grew hot enough and he filled his tin cup and sat with the cup in both hands, admiring the stars. A coyote yipped and was answered by another. Somewhere far off a grizzly roared. Closer, an owl hooted.

He turned in about midnight. His gut was so sore that it hurt to lie with his back propped on his saddle so he lay flat, his hat at his side, his arms across his chest.

The stomp of a hoof brought him around as day was breaking. It was only the Ovaro, and after he kindled the embers of his fire to life, he threw on his saddle blanket and saddle and tied on his bedroll.

Two cups drained the pot. He was sipping the last of it and

about ready to head out when a sound he'd never heard before pricked the Ovaro's ear and brought him to his feet.

It seemed to come from everywhere at once. How close, it was hard to judge. It wasn't a roar or a shriek or a howl. It was a tremendous bellow, similar to the bellows bull buffalo made when they challenged a rival for a cow's affections. But there were no buffalo that high up.

Excited, Fargo slid his tin cup into a saddlebag, forked leather, and rode up out of the gully. He drew rein and rose in the stirrups to try to catch sight of the animal responsible—and there it was, not fifty yards away, staring right at him.

"God in heaven," Fargo blurted.

Jim Tyler had said that Thunderhead was a large bull. But "large" didn't do him justice. The bull was gargantuan, taller at the shoulders and broader and more massive than the Ovaro, with a horn spread of some seven feet. It was a brindle color, dark brown with darker stripes, except around the eyes and the brow where it was almost white.

It looked to be a longhorn, although Tyler never mentioned that fact.

Fargo stared and the bull stared, and then it snorted and pawed the ground.

"Oh, hell," Fargo said.

With another of those tremendous bellows, Thunderhead lowered his head and charged.

Hauling on the reins, Fargo rode into the gully and up and out the other side and jabbed his spurs. The Ovaro didn't need much urging.

Fargo glanced back and saw Thunderhead come hurtling out of the gully and pound in pursuit. A bull that size could easily bowl the stallion over, to say nothing of the wounds those deadly horns could inflict.

A boulder loomed and Fargo avoided it. He swept up a short grade and along a bench and looked back again to see if he was increasing his lead. He wasn't.

Thunderhead was narrowing it.

Swearing, Fargo rode for dear life, the Ovaro's as much as his. He reached the end of the shelf and flew down another grade into thick timber. He figured the closely spaced trees would force Thunderhead to slow and lose ground but the bull slipped through them with a speed and agility that belied his huge size.

The Ovaro swept out of the forest and a meadow spread before them. Normally, on level ground, the stallion was uncatchable. But no one had told Thunderhead. Incredibly, the bull came on faster than ever.

Fargo lashed the Ovaro's reins even though the stallion was flying flat out.

Resembling nothing so much as a living locomotive, Thunderhead bore down on them.

Fargo began to think he might have to shoot it. Dead, the bull wasn't worth a cent, but he'd be damned if he'd let any harm come to the Ovaro.

He reached the meadow's end and plunged into more timber. Barely seconds went by and Thunderhead barreled in after him.

In addition to the drum of heavy hooves and the crash of underbrush, Fargo heard the bull's great rasps of breath. It sounded like a blacksmith's bellows.

A low limb materialized and Fargo ducked. He reined around a spruce and then around a thicket. The bull avoided the former but crashed through the latter as if it didn't exist.

Now Thunderhead was only a few yards behind them.

Fargo shot between two saplings.

Thunderhead shot between them, too, and snapped both in half as if they were twigs.

Fargo flew down a short slope and veered around a small pine that was leaning against another.

Thunderhead rammed into the pine, splintering it like so much kindling.

"Damn," Fargo fumed. The bull was damn near indestructible and determined to bring him down.

The Ovaro galloped up a short slope and out into the open again. And suddenly Fargo had a whole new problem.

He had the bull behind him.

And the Blackfeet in front of him.

29

The warriors seemed as surprised to see Fargo as he was to see them. They had heard him and the bull crashing through the forest and had drawn rein with their arrows nocked and lance arms cocked, and two who had rifles were ready to shoot.

The instant Fargo set eyes on them, he reined sharply to one side.

A rifle spanged but the Blackfoot missed. Several of the others uttered piercing war whoops and goaded their mounts toward him.

That was when Thunderhead exploded out of the trees.

The bull was close enough to the Ovaro that if it had turned, it could have gored the stallion easily. Instead, it saw the Blackfeet in its path and went straight at them. Astonishment rooted the war party. Then the other warrior with a rifle banged a shot at Thunderhead. But he rushed his shot and puffs of dust showed that the slug had hit between the bull's front legs.

Thunderhead was on them. The warrior who had just shot at the longhorn attempted to turn his horse but he wasn't anywhere near quick enough. Thunderhead slammed into the animal and both it and the warrior were smashed to earth. The horse let out a squeal while the warrior sought to scramble away from the bull.

Thunderhead had other ideas. He rammed into the warrior, knocking him flat. The Blackfoot clawed for a knife just as a horn impaled his chest. Whirling, Thunderhead went at the downed horse with the warrior's body stuck fast. A couple of head-on blows and the mangled body slipped off and the horse was still.

A warrior who was braver than the rest, or more foolhardy, bore down on the bull with his lance raised high to hurl.

An enormous lightning bolt, Thunderhead slammed into the warrior's horse and both horse and rider crashed to earth. The Blackfoot tried to spring clear but his leg was pinned. He pushed against his horse and was trying to rise when Thunderhead's horn caught him under the chin and ruptured out the back of his neck, taking part of his spine with it.

It had all happened so fast that the remaining Blackfeet were too stunned to attack together, which was their only prayer. Individually, they were no match for the massive juggernaut.

Thunderhead went after the warrior holding the lead rope to the mule and the packhorse. The man let go and sought to flee, and for once, luck was with him. The mule chose that moment to bolt, drawing Thunderhead's attention. Before the mule had gone ten feet, Thunderhead was on it.

Fargo gained cover and drew rein. He expected the bull would kill a few more but the Blackfeet made it to cover, too.

As for Thunderhead, he was going at the mule in a frenzy of butts and sweeps of his horns, and in no time at all, the mule was a broken, blood-soaked ruin.

Thunderhead straightened. Gore matted his head and horns and scarlet had splashed his brow and muzzle. He let out a bellow.

Fargo was astounded by the destruction the behemoth had wrought in so short a span. He sat his saddle perfectly still in order not to draw its attention.

Thunderhead, though, appeared to have lost interest in him. The bull went to each of the fallen warriors and sniffed them as if he was making sure they were dead.

Fargo spied the five remaining Blackfeet off through the trees. They were doing as he was doing. They were statues frozen on their mounts.

Thunderhead shook his head at the dead mule and at the dead horse, then glowered at the woods and the sky as if he were mad at the world and everything in it. Another moment, and he broke into motion, heading back the way he had come. He passed within a stone's throw of Fargo and the Ovaro without seeing them.

Fargo didn't move until the bull was out of sight. He waited half a minute to be certain and was debating what to do when he saw that the Blackfeet were spreading out and moving toward him.

From the frying pan into the fire and back again, Fargo realized. He reined after Thunderhead and followed him, staying a good thirty yards back.

The Blackfeet, as he'd hoped, didn't give chase. They'd had enough of the mad bull and didn't care to come anywhere near it.

Fargo was worried that Thunderhead would hear the Ovaro and turn. But the bull lumbered on, oblivious, almost as if it had somewhere it hankered to be.

Fargo followed for a short way farther to be sure about the Blackfeet, then reined to the west and as quietly as possible got the hell out of there.

He didn't feel safe until he'd gone half a mile.

Climbing to a bald crown where he could see in all directions, he slid off and patted the Ovaro.

"Damn," he said.

That had been close. It could easily have been him the longhorn gored.

Returning Thunderhead for the bounty had taken on a whole new dimension. Hearing that the bull had gored someone couldn't compare to seeing the monster in action. Anyone who tried to rope that bull put their life in their hands.

Fargo had figured to toss a noose over him and lead Thunderhead back without much difficulty. He'd handled bulls before. But Thunderhead was no ordinary animal. He was a force of nature in and of himself.

"Damn," Fargo said once more.

So now he had the remaining Blackfeet to worry about and the Hollisters were still out there and there was the mystery killer who was exterminating the bull hunters—and the bull, itself.

"What the hell have I gotten myself into?"

As if in answer, from out of the labyrinth of canyons and bluffs to the northwest rose another defiant bellow.

30

Fargo wasn't the only one who heard that bellow.

He was indulging in rare midday cups of coffee when out of the trees rode Dirk Peters.

Peters climbed down and chuckled and said, "Is this your notion of bull-hunting? Sitting on your ass?"

Fargo grinned. "After what I've been through, it's sure as hell the safest."

"You've seen him?"

"Pull up a cup," Fargo said, and when Peters made himself comfortable, he related his encounter.

"The bull *and* the Blackfeet," Dirk said. "You don't do things by half."

"There's more," Fargo said, and told him about the farmer and the old woman and the other two he found, ending with, "Someone has killed four of us so far and likely won't stop there."

"Six of us," Dirk said. "I came across two more my own self. One had been stabbed and the other was shot in the back."

"Backshooters," Fargo said in disgust.

"This hunt has gone to hell," Dirk said, "and will likely get worse." He thoughtfully tapped his tin cup with a fingernail. "It gives a man something to think about."

"Oh?"

"I haven't seen this bull yet but I did find some old tracks. Which is why I don't think you're telling a tall tale when you say he's about the biggest damn bull who ever screwed a cow. And if he's that big and that mean, he might be more than one gent can handle."

"Might be," Fargo admitted.

"So how about if I take a look-see and if he's all he sounds like he is, we consider partnering up." Dirk held up a hand before Fargo went to speak. "I know you probably want the five thousand for yourself. But half is better than an empty poke"—he paused—"or being dead."

"I'm fond of breathing," Fargo said.

"Is that a yes?"

"You can have your look-see and we'll decide then."

They spent the next hour and a half searching in the direction of that last bellow. For some reason Thunderhead preferred the maze of canyons and bluffs to an open meadow or the timber.

"Easier for him to hide," Dirk Peters remarked when Fargo mentioned it. "Which fits with him being longhorn. I've heard they hide out in the roughest country they can find."

"There's plenty of it here," Fargo said.

"Cows and bulls," Dirk said. "You couldn't pay me enough to wet-nose those stupid critters." He paused. "I've been to Texas. Folks down there say longhorns aren't only quick and tough, they're uncommon smart. Corralling this Thunderhead won't be easy."

"You don't need to tell me."

"What we have is a bull as big as a mountain with the disposition of a kicked rattler and horns he could shove down our throat and have poke out our ass."

Fargo laughed. "You have a colorful way of putting things."

"Just so he doesn't put one of those horns in me."

Presently they rounded a bluff and ahead trickled a ribbon of blue, issuing from the mouth of a canyon.

"What have we here?" Dirk said with sudden interest.

Fargo had seen them, too. Tracks. A lot of them. He dismounted and held on to the Ovaro's reins as he sank to a knee. "Fresh ones and old ones," he said. "Going in and coming out."

"By God," Dirk said, "we've found his hidey-hole."

It was some hole. The canyon had to be a quarter-mile across and the rock walls were some of the highest Fargo ever set eyes on. Thanks to the stream, the canyon floor had plenty of grass and trees and thick brush.

"He could be in there looking at us right this minute and we wouldn't know it," Dirk said.

"Maybe there's a way to the top," Fargo said. "We can spy on him from above."

"If there is, it could take an hour or more to find it and another hour for the climb," Dirk said. "I vote we seize the bull by the horns." He grinned at his wit.

"This bull-hunting isn't for the timid," Fargo said.

They warily advanced, Fargo on one side of the stream, Dirk on the other. Tracks were everywhere. So was evidence the grass had been cropped. And a tree bore rub marks where the bull had scratched itself.

"Home sweet home," Dirk joked.

The dense thickets posed a problem. A bull standing still, even a bull the size of Thunderhead, would be hard to spot.

Fargo looked for the telltale flick of an ear or the swish of a tail but all he saw were several sparrows and butterflies.

"It's damned pretty here," Dirk said.

Fargo wished he would hush. Longhorns had keen hearing. And you wouldn't think that something that weighed a ton or more could sneak up on a man, but they were ghosts when they wanted to be.

"There!" Dirk whispered, and drew rein and pointed.

Fargo stopped. He stared at the thicket Dirk was pointing at and for the life of him couldn't see anything. Then an ear twitched, and suddenly an enormous silhouette took shape.

"The critter blends right in," Dirk marveled.

"We should back off," Fargo advised. He had been charged enough for one day.

"I want a better look."

"He might come after you."

"Just a little closer," Dirk said, and clucked to his zebra dun.

The silhouette in the thicket rumbled like distant thunder.

"Don't," Fargo warned.

Dirk stopped but the harm had been done.

Out of the thicket exploded Thunderhead.

31

Fargo reined around to get the hell out of there.

Dirk Peters, though, was transfixed with astonishment. He sat there gawking as the bull rapidly gained speed, snorting angrily.

"Fan the breeze, damn it!" Fargo hollered.

His yell galvanized Peters into yanking on his reins and jabbing his heels.

The three hundred yards to the canyon mouth were some of the longest of Fargo's life. He raced out and bore to the north with Dirk not far behind. They went a goodly distance with their heads turned, expecting Thunderhead to come rushing out after them.

Another minute, and Fargo brought the Ovaro to a halt and Dirk Peters followed suit.

"Was that a close enough look for you?" Fargo asked.

"Jesus God Almighty," Dirk exclaimed. "He's bigger than a griz."

"We were damned lucky he let us go."

"No wonder that rancher is so set on having him back," Dirk said. "As breeding stock, that critter is worth his weight in gold."

"And mean as hell."

Dirk pushed his hat back on his head and rubbed his chin. "I don't see him letting us lead him to the ranch as gentle as a lamb."

Fargo snorted.

"How in hell are we going to do this?"

"Carefully," Fargo said.

"I've changed my mind," Dirk said. "Let's look for a way to the top. I'd like to see the lay of that canyon. Maybe it will give us an idea of how to go about it."

A series of boulder-strewn slopes brought them to where they wanted to be, high atop the north canyon wall. Taking off their hats, they flattened and crawled to the brink and peered over.

"I'll be damned," Dirk said. "He picked himself an oasis."

The canyon narrowed about midway and curved to the south. Past the bend the stream was wider. Its source was a spring that had formed a pond. There was enough grass to provide graze for fifty bulls, and acres of thickets.

"I don't see him," Dirk said.

Nor did Fargo.

"As huge as he is, how can he hide so good?"

Fargo had known grizzlies to conceal themselves so they were impossible to spot. It was no surprise the bull could do the same. "What we need to work out is how to catch him."

Dirk snapped his fingers. "I know. We get him to chase us all the way down to the ranch."

"Be serious."

Dirk chuckled. "If you don't like my brainstorm, let's hear yours."

"I don't have one."

"Well, damn. I hate to be licked by a bull."

Fargo hated to be licked by anyone or anything but this had him stumped. He was studying on how to perform their miracle when Dirk stirred and said, "Uh-oh," and pointed.

"Is that who I think it is?"

A rider wearing a wide-brimmed black hat was entering the canyon.

"Rafer Crown," Fargo said.

The bounty hunter was paralleling the stream. Bent low from his saddle, he was intently studying the ground. He glanced ahead once and then back at the canyon mouth.

"He sees our tracks," Dirk said. "He knows two riders went in and came out again."

Fargo was watching for Thunderhead and was rewarded with a glimpse of brindle over in a thicket at the bottom of the far canyon wall. It was his turn to point. "The bull has seen him."

"If we yell to warn Rafer, it might provoke the critter into charging."

"If we don't warn him," Fargo said, "Thunderhead will wait until Crown is so close he can't get away."

"Damn it to hell." Dirk suddenly stood and cupped his hands to his mouth. "Rafer! Get out of there! The critter has seen you!"

The bounty hunter drew rein and looked up.

"Get out of there!" Dirk repeated. "The bull! The bull!"

Fargo stood and extended an arm at the far wall.

Crown shifted in his saddle just as the longhorn broke out of the shadows at a full charge. Crown's hands swept to his pistols and he drew them with flashing speed.

"He's going to shoot it!" Dirk exclaimed.

Crown hesitated, then spun the revolvers into their holsters, grabbed his reins, and wheeled his bay. A rake of his spurs sent the horse fleeing down the canyon with Thunderhead hurtling after them.

"He's not going to make it," Dirk said. "We have to do something."

What could they do, Fargo realized, other than try to shoot Thunderhead? And that high up, with the bull moving so fast, they'd be lucky to hit it, let alone bring it down.

"God," Dirk said. "The critter is gaining."

Thunderhead had cut the distance by more than half. For something so huge, the bull was incredibly fast.

The bounty hunter was whipping his reins like a madman. He looked back and saw that Thunderhead was closing.

Fargo wondered if Crown would shoot rather than have his horse be bowled over and gored. He would, if it was the Ovaro.

Seconds of tense dread ensued. Then, unexpectedly, Thunderhead slowed and stopped and stood tossing his horns as Rafer Crown fled out of the canyon to safety.

"Wheeooo!" Dirk happily declared. "That bounty hunter is one lucky coon. The same as we were."

The thing with luck, though, Fargo mused, was that no one's held forever.

32

Rafer Crown was waiting when they descended. He'd got a fire going in an open space a safe distance from the canyon mouth and put a pot of coffee on and was seated on a log he'd dragged over, chewing jerky. "Thanks for the holler," he said as they dismounted. "That damn brute almost had me."

"Almost had us, too," Dirk Peters said. He sank down cross-legged with his elbows on his knees and his chin in his hands.

"I caught sight of five Blackfeet earlier," Crown mentioned. "They appeared to be hunting someone."

"That would be me," Fargo said as he eased to the ground.

"Come across any dead bull hunters?" Dirk asked the bounty man.

"I have, in fact," Crown said. "A storekeeper who had his throat slit."

"How do you know he was a storekeeper?"

"I went through his saddlebags."

"Was anything taken?" Fargo asked. "His guns? His horse?"

Crown shook his head. "His horse was there and he had a rifle beside him."

"Then it wasn't the war party," Dirk said. "No Blackfoot in his right mind would pass up a gun or a horse."

Fargo and Peters told Crown about the bodies they'd found, and Fargo gave a brief account of his run-in with the Hollisters.

"You've had it worse than me," Crown said. "The only difficulty I've had was that bull."

"Skye and me were thinking of joining forces," Dirk Peters revealed. "How would you two feel about a three-way split?"

"I don't know," Crown said.

"You've got your heart set on the full five thousand," Dirk said, nodding. "I don't blame you. I did too. But my pa taught me to use my head, and tackling that bull by my lonesome is the same as sticking one foot in an early grave."

"I still don't know," Crown said.

"Ponder on it some. Take all night," Dirk said. "I don't reckon that ornery bull is going anywhere."

"There's four or five hours of daylight left," Crown observed. "I'd hate to waste it."

"You're welcome to go try and catch the bull by yourself," Dirk said. "We'll bury what's left after he's done goring and stomping."

"There has to be a way," Crown said.

"I'm all ears."

Fargo noticed that the Ovaro had raised its head and was staring down the mountain. He looked and said, "We're about to have company."

Glyn and Aramone Richmond were climbing toward them. Aramone rose in her stirrups to wave.

"Hell," Dirk said. "This mountain is damn crowded."

"We're all after the same animal," Crown said. "We're bound to bump into each other."

"I know what I'd like to bump against," Dirk said, grinning and winking and thrusting his hips.

"That gal is right pretty," Crown said. "But she's not likely to fool around with her brother along."

"What do you think, Skye?" Dirk asked.

"You never know with females," Fargo said dryly.

As the Easterners came closer, Fargo noticed that Glyn's suit was as spotless as it had been at the ranch, while Aramone's dress didn't have a speck of dust. She rode sidesaddle and was twirling her parasol across her shoulder.

"Will you look at them," Dirk Peters declared. "They're clean enough to eat off of."

"That was a silly thing to say," Crown said. "Who eats people?"

Fargo coughed.

"They might as well be strolling down a street," Dirk said.

"They won't do any strolling when that bull lights after them," Crown said.

Fargo stood and stepped around the fire to greet them.

"We meet again," Glyn said. "Had any luck? We know the bull is close by somewhere."

"Closer than you think, dandy man," Dirk said, and laughed.

"We're holding a bull-hunters convention," Fargo said to Aramone. "Care to join us?" He held up his arms to help her down.

"Aren't you the gallant gentleman," she replied, playfully batting her eyelashes. Sliding off, she pressed flush with his chest and legs while smiling in seeming innocence.

Fargo felt himself stir, and stepped back. "Had any trouble?"

"There was a fly that was bothersome," Aramone said.

Dirk let out with a bleat of amusement. "Lady, pretty near half of the people who started out after Thunderhead have been murdered and all you've had to fret about was a fly?"

"What was that about murder?" Glyn said.

Once again Fargo had to recite all that had happened. When he was done, it was Dirk's turn. Rafer Crown mentioned that he'd found "a dead one" and that was it.

"And you say the bull is in that canyon?" Glyn said, staring off.

"Is that all you can think of?" Dirk said. "Didn't you hear us about all the folks who have been killed?"

"I heard you fine," Glyn said, "but they don't mean anything to me. I didn't know any of them."

"How about you, lady?" Dirk said. "You don't look broke up about them, either."

"Why should I shed a tear over complete strangers?" Aramone replied.

"At least you could frown in their memory, you silly hen," Dirk said.

Glyn Richmond colored with resentment. "Be careful how you address my sister."

"Or what?" Dirk bristled. "You'll beat me to death with your bowler?"

"I have half a mind to thrash you," Glyn said.

"Commence if you are man enough," Dirk taunted.

It was then that Rafer Crown got their attention by loudly clearing his throat. "If you two infants can stop your squabbling, there's someone else who wants to join our party."

"Who?" Dirk said.

Rafer extended an arm at the canyon. "Not who," he said. "What."

It was Thunderhead.

33

Fargo had been running his eyes over Aramone and thinking how nice it would be to go for a stroll later. He was as surprised as everyone else to discover that Thunderhead had emerged from the canyon and was staring at them.

"God Almighty!" Glyn Richmond exclaimed. "Look at the size of him."

"That's what I said," Aramone said, and gave Fargo a wink the others didn't catch.

"I didn't hear you say it," Dirk Peters said.

Rafer Crown had risen and was sidling toward his bay. "We'd best light a shuck while we can."

"Hold on," Dirk said. "Look yonder."

Thunderhead had turned and was walking away in the opposite direction.

"He's not going to try and kill us?" Dirk said in amazement.

"Longhorns are like buffalo," Rafer Crown said. "They're as unpredictable as hell."

"The same as people," Aramone said.

"This is our chance. We should go after him," Glyn excitedly proposed. "He's out in the open. Even big as he is, he should be easy to catch."

"You go right ahead," Dirk said, "and I will laugh when we bury you."

"There are five of us," Glyn said. "That should be enough."

"Mister, have you ever tried to rope a bull?" Dirk asked.

"No."

"Have you ever even roped a cow?"

"I'm no farmer or rancher."

"It takes a knack. And what do you reckon Thunderhead will be doing while we're trying to toss a loop over him? I'll tell you. He'll

97

be trying his damnedest to gore us and our horses. Which will make roping him that much harder."

"I never said anything about using a rope," Glyn said.

"How else?" Dirk said. "Are you fixing to walk up to him and say, 'Pretty please, come with me'?"

Rafer Crown laughed.

"There has to be a way," Glyn said.

"I'm all ears," Dirk told him.

Fargo hadn't taken his eyes off Thunderhead. The bull was almost out of sight. On an impulse, he stepped to the Ovaro and swung up.

"Where the blazes are you going?" Dirk Peters wanted to know.

"I'd like a look at that canyon." Fargo was curious about why the bull kept coming back to it.

"We already had one," Dirk said, "and nearly got killed, remember?"

"I want another look anyway."

"Suit yourself. But once was enough for me."

Thunderhead had disappeared around a bluff.

Fargo reined past the fire but stopped when Rafer Crown said his name.

"I'll tag along if you don't mind," the bounty hunter offered.

"We all should go," Aramone said.

"The fewer, the better," Fargo said. "Stay out here and fire a couple of shots if you see him coming back."

"That we can do," Dirk said.

Crown brought his bay alongside the Ovaro and nodded, and together they trotted to the canyon. As they started up it, Crown said, "In case you're wondering why I came, when I go after a bounty, I like to learn all I can about the man I'm after. What he wears. What he likes. What he does. His haunts." Crown gestured at the high walls. "A good hunter does that whether what he's after has two legs or four."

That was the most the bounty hunter had said to Fargo since they met. It prompted him to say, "I take it you go after bounties for the hunt as much as the money."

"The money makes it worth my while," Crown said, "but you're right. It's the hunt I care about. I get a thrill I wouldn't get clerking in some store."

Fargo was examining the ground as they went. He had stuck

close to the stream but now he reined wide and roved back and forth.

Crown stayed with him. "What are you looking for?"

"I'm getting a feel for his habits."

"Like where he beds down? Are you figuring to jump him in his sleep?" Crown chuckled.

They came to where the canyon narrowed and went around the bend.

Fargo was beginning to think he was wasting his time when he spotted something that brought him to a stop.

"What?" Crown said.

Dismounting, Fargo sank to a knee. "Look at these."

More hoofprints. But not Thunderhead's. These were considerably smaller. There were a lot of them, and they led from the stream to the acres of thicket and back again.

"A cow?" Crown said in surprise. "He's got company up here?"

"He may have more than that." Fargo swung back on the Ovaro and rode slowly toward the thicket.

A trail in and out had been flattened by the repeated passage of the canyon's new occupants.

Drawing rein again, Fargo alighted and held his reins out to the bounty hunter. "We need to know for sure."

"If you hear their shots, you come running," Crown said.

The path of crushed vegetation was as wide as Thunderhead. Dry, broken stems crunched with every step Fargo took, but it couldn't be helped.

It brought him to the middle where half an acre had been trampled flat. Crouching so he wouldn't be seen, he peered out.

And there, her legs tucked under her and peacefully chewing her cud, was a brindle cow. Beside her, dozing, was a calf.

"I'll be damned," Fargo said under his breath. He recollected the rancher telling him about a heifer the bull had been partial to, and how Tyler used the heifer to lead the longhorn along like a little kitten. This must be the same heifer, Fargo realized, only now that she'd given birth, she was more rightly called a cow.

It explained why Thunderhead was so protective of the canyon. The bull regarded anyone who came near his family as a threat.

The very next moment, the high walls echoed to the boom of gunfire.

34

The others were firing warning shots.

Thunderhead must be returning.

Whirling, Fargo ran. He was only halfway when more shots boomed. It must be Dirk's way of letting them know the bull was close and they'd better get the hell out of there.

Rafer Crown had turned his bay and was staring down the canyon. "About time," he grumbled.

Without breaking stride, Fargo vaulted up. A rake of his spurs and they raced to the bend and around it into the wider part of the canyon.

Below, just entering, was Thunderhead. The bull stopped at seeing them and raised its head.

Fargo and Crown both drew rein.

"Wonderful," the bounty hunter said. "He has us trapped."

Fargo sat perfectly still. He was trying not to do anything that would provoke the longhorn. Thunderhead stared and they stared back and then Thunderhead snorted and stomped a front hoof.

"Oh, hell," Crown said. "From now on I stick to two-legged bounties."

With a bellow that shook the canyon walls, Thunderhead charged. Dirt and stones flew out from under his driving hooves and he raised a cloud of dust in his wake.

Crown raised his reins but Fargo said, "Not yet. Wait until I say. You go right and I'll go left."

"I don't much like letting that critter get close," Crown said.

Fargo didn't like the idea, either. He was hoping Thunderhead was more concerned with the cow and the calf than with wanting to kill them. If not, either or both of them would pay for his hunch with their lives.

The bull had his head low, his horns and thick brow thrust

forward. His nostrils flared with every breath and his eyes were pits of rage.

"Not yet," Fargo said when Crown went to rein aside.

"I hope you know what we're doing."

Fargo barely heard him. The pounding of Thunderhead's hooves nearly drowned him out. By now the bull was close enough that Fargo could see dried blood from the Blackfeet it had killed on the tips of its horns.

Thirty feet separated them and then twenty feet and Fargo bawled, "Now!"

He yanked on the reins and the Ovaro turned and for an awful moment Fargo thought he had been too slow. Then Thunderhead swept past, the tip of his horn not an inch from the Ovaro.

Fargo didn't waste another second. He raked his spurs and didn't slow until the canyon was behind them.

"What was in that thicket, anyhow?" Crown asked.

Fargo told him.

"This might make it easier."

"It might," Fargo agreed.

"Or it might make some of us dead."

"That too."

Dirk and Aramone were anxiously waiting. Glyn, on the other hand, looked disappointed that they were alive.

"I shot as soon as I saw him," Dirk said.

"You did good," Fargo said as he dismounted.

"I was so worried," Aramone said. "The bull didn't try to kill you?"

"He did," Fargo replied. "But he had something else on his mind and we were able to get away."

"What else?" Glyn Richmond asked.

Fargo told them about the cow and the calf.

Dirk Peters let out a cackle. "It must be true love." He laughed and slapped his legs. "This puts us in the saddle if we do it right."

"What the hell are you talking about?" Glyn Richmond asked.

"You Easterners," Dirk said with ill-disguised scorn, "don't know diddly."

"I know I don't like you looking down your nose at me," Glyn said.

"Brother, please," Aramone said.

"He treats us like we're simpletons," Glyn said. "You heard him while they were gone."

Fargo looked at Dirk.

"All I said was that they'd have been smart to stay east of the Mississippi. They are fish out of water out here."

"You didn't call us fish," Glyn said. "You called us jackasses."

"I was thinking fish," Dirk said.

"I've had enough of you," Glyn Richmond said and punched Dirk Peters in the mouth.

35

Dirk Peters unleashed a left cross to the jaw that rocked Glyn back a step.

"Stop it!" Aramone cried, but neither man paid attention.

Suddenly they were slugging toe to toe.

Fargo didn't intervene. The pair had been prickly toward each other since they met. This was bound to happen sooner or later.

Rafer Crown made no move to separate them, either. All he did was say, "This should be interesting."

They were evenly matched. Glyn appeared to have some skill at boxing but Dirk had faster reflexes and his punches, when they landed, were solid. Glyn caught him with a body blow and he retaliated with a loop to the temple that knocked Glyn's bowler off.

"Someone stop them," Aramone pleaded. "Please."

"They're grown men," Crown said. "Or they're supposed to be."

Aramone looked at Fargo. "For me."

"If either pulls a gun I will."

"I'd let them shoot each other," Crown said.

The pair went at it in grim earnest. Circling, feinting, jabbing, swinging, each scored but did little real harm.

"I've seen girls who fought better," Rafer Crown remarked.

"Go to hell," Aramone said. "My brother is doing fine."

"They might as well be dancing," Crown said.

"I'd like to see you do half as good."

"I don't fight with my fists."

"What then? Knives?"

Crown placed his hands on his pistols. "What do you think?"

The next moment Glyn clipped Dirk on the cheek and Dirk nailed him in the gut. Glyn doubled over, putting his jaw in easy reach, and Dirk drew back his fist to end it.

Suddenly Dirk jerked as if from an invisible punch and clutched at his shoulder. Far off, a rifle cracked.

"Everyone down!" Fargo hollered and flung himself at Aramone, pulling her with him.

Crown flattened, too, but Dirk was standing with a hand pressed to his shoulder, looking bewildered.

Glyn Richmond was confused, too. Gazing about, he blurted, "What? What is it?"

Fargo dived at both men. They were close enough that he got an arm around the legs of each and upended them with a twist of his shoulders.

Glyn cursed and Dirk squawked and then they were on the ground and Fargo yelled, "Someone is shooting at us, you idiots."

Glyn forgot all about Dirk. His hand whipped under his jacket and reappeared holding his pocket pistol. "Where?" he said.

"They're too far off."

Fargo saw blood trickling from between Dirk's fingers and asked, "How bad?"

"Can't tell yet," Dirk answered, grimacing. "But it hurts like hell."

"Stay down," Fargo commanded. "All of you." He snaked to the Ovaro, crabbed around to the other side, and quickly slid his Henry from the saddle scabbard.

Judging by the sound of the shot, it had come from hundreds of yards off. Fargo focused on a bluff as the likely spot. From up top, whoever it was had a clear view of them and their fire. He trained the Henry but saw no movement.

"We're too exposed," Crown said. Like Fargo, he was staring at the bluff.

Swinging onto the Ovaro, Fargo pointed his Henry at a belt of firs. "Get into those trees and see to Peters."

"What will you be doing?" Glyn Richmond asked.

"What the hell do you think?" Fargo replied, and tapped his spurs. He'd gain them the time they needed to hunt cover by making a target of himself.

Hunching low, he crisscrossed back and forth, expecting at any second to hear the crack of another shot. He reached the bluff and drew rein. It was too sheer on this side for a man to climb. The shooter had to have found another way up. Keeping watch on the rim, he rode around to the far side. An incline brought him to the crest.

No one was there. A few boulders, several small scrub brush, and that was it.

Fargo scoured the terrain beyond. Again, there was no sign of anyone. No riders. No retreating figures. Nothing.

He moved to where he was sure the shooter must have been but there were no footprints, no evidence a body had lain there, not so much as a scrape mark. He searched to either side, but once again, nothing.

Shaking his head, Fargo expressed his puzzlement with, "What the hell?"

36

Rafer Crown had kindled a fire and put water on to boil. Aramone was tending to Dirk Peters while Glyn stood guard with a rifle. Their horses and the pack animals were tied to nearby trees.

"I didn't hear shots," Crown commented as Fargo swung down.

"There was no sign of the shooter."

"Did you follow their tracks?" Crown asked.

"No tracks, either."

"That's not possible," the bounty hunter said. "Everyone leaves sign."

"Apaches don't."

"This ain't Apache country." Crown stared toward the bluff. "If it was anyone else, I'd figure they couldn't track worth beans. But you're one of the best scouts alive, or so folks say."

"A clever shooter could do it," Fargo said. "Wrap, say, rabbit fur around their feet."

"Then use another piece to wipe away any trace?" Crown nodded. "I've seen it done before. The rub marks usually give it away."

"There weren't any." Fargo thought of Humphries and Esther and the other bodies. "This killer isn't stupid."

Dirk Peters had peeled his buckskin shirt from his shoulder and was lying propped against a log. He had overheard and said, "Stupid or smart, as soon as I'm able to hunt him, he's dead. No one shoots me and gets away with it."

"You won't be going anywhere for a while," Aramone said as she carefully probed at the entry hole. "I have to dig this slug out."

"I can do it," Fargo offered.

"I know how," Aramone said. "I've done it before, and I'm not squeamish."

"You shouldn't be helping him," her brother said. "He took a swing at me, remember?"

"The fight is over," Aramone said. "And you swung first, as I recall."

"You're my sister," Glyn said. "You're supposed to side with me."

"I will when you're in the right but I'm helping him and that's final."

Rafer Crown hooked his thumbs in his gun belt. "Enough of this damn bickering."

"No one asked you," Glyn said. "I'll thank you to keep your nose out of our business."

"When I have to listen to it, you make it my business, too. And it stops, now."

"I'm warning you," Glyn said.

"I told your sister and now I'll tell you," Crown said. "I'm not Peters. Treat me like you treat him and she can bury you."

Glyn Richmond started to level his rifle.

With a lightning flick, Crown's Remington Navy was in his hand, pointed at Glyn's belly.

Richmond froze.

"You try that again and you're dead," Crown said flatly.

"Glyn, please," Aramone said. "You're not helping matters."

"My own sister," Glyn said angrily. Jerking his rifle down, he marched off into the trees.

"Damned yak," Crown growled.

"We're sure a friendly bunch," Dirk Peters said, and laughed.

Fargo didn't find it nearly as hilarious. They had enough to worry about without clawing at each other. "What will you use to dig out the slug?"

"I hadn't thought that far ahead," Aramone said.

Tucking at the waist, Fargo palmed his Arkansas toothpick. "Use this."

Aramone tested its edges with a finger and nodded in satisfaction. "It's as sharp as anything."

"A dull knife isn't much use."

Soon the water was hot. Aramone cleaned the wound using a cloth from her packhorse, then delicately probed with the toothpick.

To his credit, Dirk didn't let out a peep. He grit his teeth and bore the pain, only squirming once when she must have hit a nerve.

Aramone inserted the blade a third of the way before she found the slug. By twisting and prying, she succeeded in forcing it far enough out that she used the tips of two fingers to work it the rest of the way. She held the blood-wet lead to the sunlight and said, "Here you go."

"Give it to me," Dirk said, holding out his other hand.

"What do you want it for?"

"As a keepsake. I have an arrowhead in my saddle bags from the time a Lakota warrior put an arrow in my leg."

"You might get another arrow in you before this is done," Rafer Crown said.

"Why say a thing like that?" Aramone asked.

Crown gestured at a point out past the firs. "The Blackfeet are back."

37

Fargo had already seen them.

Five warriors had appeared to the south. The one in the lead was tracking, and they were heading toward the mouth of the canyon.

"They're out for revenge for the ones the bull killed," Rafer Crown guessed.

Aramone rose for a better look. "How can you possibly know that?"

"It's what I'd do if I was in their moccasins," Crown said.

Fargo agreed with the bounty hunter. The Blackfeet didn't raise cattle. The only use they had for a cow or bull was to eat it, and even then they preferred buffalo. Buffs were everything to them: food, shelter, weapons, tools. Cow meat tasted strange and the hides weren't nearly as useful.

"If they kill Thunderhead," Dirk Peters said, "there goes the five thousand dollars."

"I reckon I can't allow that," Crown said.

"For once I'm with you," Glyn Richmond said. "Let's go deal with them."

"Skye?" Crown said.

Fargo had no quarrel with the Blackfeet. He didn't want them killing the longhorn, either. "We drive them off without killing them if we can."

"Why go to that much trouble?" Glyn said. "We have rifles. We can pick them off from a distance and that will be the end of it."

"No killing," Fargo said.

Glyn shook his head in disgust. "You frontier types aren't anything like I expected. Just the fact they're Indians should be enough excuse for us to kill them."

"Not all of us out here are like you," Dirk said.

"And how am I?" Glyn responded.

"You're— What's the word?" Dirk pretended to think a moment. "A damned bigot."

"I despise their kind. I admit it," Glyn said. "How many whites have they slaughtered and scalped over the years?"

"They scalp anyone you know?" Dirk asked.

"What's that have to do with anything?"

Fargo moved to the Ovaro and climbed on. Reining over to Aramone he said, "Stay here and look after Peters. Dirk, keep your guns handy. Any trouble, fire three shots into the air."

"Will do, general," Peters said, smirking.

"My sister goes with me," Glyn said.

"I can't," Aramone said. "I'm not done bandaging Mr. Peters."

"I don't like it," Glyn said.

"What can he do, hurt as he is?" Aramone said. "Besides, he's been a perfect gentleman all this time."

"Wait," Dirk said. "Are you saying what I think you're saying?"

Fargo sighed and gigged the Ovaro. Crown had mounted, too, and quickly caught up.

"Are you as tired of it as I am?"

"I could do without," Fargo said.

"For two bits I'd goad the brother into going for his six-shooter but it would likely upset the sister."

"You think?" Fargo said.

They rode out of the firs and made straight for the warriors. They hadn't gone far when Glyn Richmond trotted up on Fargo's left.

"You should have waited for me."

Fargo didn't say anything.

"How do you want to do this?"

"I'm going to ask them to leave," Fargo said.

Glyn looked at him, incredulous. "They'll put an arrow or a bullet into you before you can get close enough. I refuse to be so foolish."

"Go back then," Fargo said, hoping he would.

They rode a little farther and Glyn said, "No. My sister will never forgive me if you come to harm and I didn't try to help you."

The Blackfeet hadn't noticed them yet but would soon. The tracker was reading sign and the others were watching him. Then one glanced up, thrust his arm out, and said something that caused the rest to turn and hold their weapons ready for use.

"They've seen us," Glyn declared.

"Easterners don't miss much," Crown said.

"Don't you start on me, too," Glyn said. "I've had enough of it from Peters."

"Quiet," Fargo said.

The tracker had climbed back on his warhorse and the five Blackfeet were looking at one another as if unsure what to do.

"We could drop them easy," Glyn said. "You're making a mistake."

"Crown?" Fargo said.

The bounty hunter looked at him.

"If he tries anything, shoot him."

"Gladly," Crown said.

Glyn opened his mouth but thought better of it and stayed silent.

"This is as far as you two go," Fargo said. They slowed and stopped and he rode on, but slowly. When he was close enough for the Blackfeet to plainly see, he held his right hand up to his neck, palm out, with his first two fingers pointed at the sky, and raised his hand until his fingers were level with his nose. It was sign language for "friend."

None of the warriors responded.

Fargo did it again. He was encouraged by the fact that the two warriors with single-shot rifles weren't pointing them at him, and a warrior with a bow had an arrow nocked but hadn't drawn back the string.

Fargo drew rein about twenty feet out. He made the sign for friend again and waited for them to show their intentions.

Then the tracker pointed at him and held two fingers to the right of his mouth and moved his hand to the left.

It was sign language for "You lie."

38

Fargo half expected the warriors to attack but they didn't. He held his right hand under his chin with his index finger straight out, the sign for "I speak with a straight tongue."

The tracker gazed past him at Crown and Richmond and surprised Fargo by saying, "Me talk white tongue." He held his thumb and first finger about half an inch apart, a white gesture, not sign language. "Little bit."

Fargo knew a smattering of Blackfoot but not enough to say what he now did in English, "My friends and I have no fight with the Blackfeet. We would have you go in peace."

"Not go," the warrior said. He rested his lance across his horse, pointed at the canyon, then raised both hands to the sides of his head with his first fingers slightly crooked to resemble horns. It was the sign for "buffalo" but he was referring to Thunderhead. "We kill."

"We have come to take the bull back to where it comes from," Fargo said. "We do not want it dead."

"It kill friends."

"I know," Fargo said. "I was there."

"Bull must die."

Fargo racked his brain for some way of persuading them to let it be. If they had a pipe he'd offer to smoke it with them. Maybe then they'd believe that he sincerely desired to be their friend.

But the next instant another tremendous bellow rent the air and out of the canyon hurtled a ton or more of enraged longhorn.

A warrior with a rifle snapped it to his shoulder and fired. The others started to scatter except for the warrior with the lance, who reined toward Thunderhead, uttered a war whoop, and slapped his heels to his horse.

"No!" Fargo yelled, but he was wasting his breath. Things had gone to hell and there was no stopping it.

The young warrior with the lance displayed foolhardy courage. He rose with the lance and let fly. Unfortunately, it glanced off a horn, and before the young warrior could rein around to flee, Thunderhead slammed into his warhorse with the impact of a train engine.

The horse squealed as it went down. The warrior tried to leap clear and was caught full on the bull's head.

It was the same as being smashed with a sledgehammer.

Fargo heard the crack of ribs and saw blood spurt from the warrior's mouth and nose.

In a twinkling the bull whirled after the others.

A warrior with a bow shifted and unleashed a shaft. It hit the bony ridge across the longhorn's brow and was deflected.

The Blackfeet did the only thing they could. They fled with the bull thundering after them.

Fargo sat and watched until they were out of sight. An idea had taken hold. It would work only if the bull was gone a spell, and it appeared that Thunderhead was determined to chase the Blackfeet to the ends of creation. There might never be a better chance.

Reining toward the canyon, Fargo motioned at Crown and Richmond. He didn't wait for them but galloped up the canyon, unlimbering his rope as he went. He wasn't a cowhand but he'd worked with cattle and could toss a loop fairly well.

He figured he'd need to sneak into the thicket and surprise the cow as she was chewing her cud. But when he came around the bend, there she was, her and the calf both, drinking at the pond.

The cow raised her head and turned to face him. Instinctively, the calf moved behind her for protection.

Fargo slowed and moved to put himself between the stream and thicket.

She was the same brindle color as Thunderhead but she wasn't nearly as big and her horns were shorter and curved forward at the ends. Getting a rope over her would be easier than over her mate.

Hooves pounded, and Rafer Crown and Glyn Richmond appeared.

The cow turned so she faced both Fargo and the new arrivals.

Crown had a brief exchange with Richmond and the Easterner

nodded and stayed at the bend, no doubt to keep the cow from flee-ing down the canyon.

Not that she looked disposed to take flight. Longhorn females weren't timid. This one tossed her head in anger and stomped a hoof.

Crown came partway and stopped. "Both or you?" he hollered.

"I'll try first," Fargo said. "Be ready if she gets past me."

A poke of his spurs, and Fargo galloped toward the cow. He swung his rope, the loop open and wide.

The cow didn't wait for him to come to her. She thrust her horns out and barreled at the Ovaro.

Fargo waited until the last possible moment and reined aside even as he threw. The cow missed her charge but he didn't. The rope settled over her horns and head and slipped onto her neck as neatly as could be. Quickly, he dallied it around the saddle horn and braced for the shock.

The lasso went taut and the cow came to a stop so abruptly, her legs nearly swept out from under her.

She managed to stay upright and stood shaking her head and straining against the rope.

The stallion knew to brace against her weight. All Fargo had to do was keep the lariat taut. "Crown!" he yelled. "The calf! We can save us a lot of trouble."

Crown understood. He veered his bay toward it.

This whole time, the calf hadn't moved except to raise its head and bawl. It wanted its mother. It still didn't move when Crown brought his bay to a sliding stop and sprang down. Only then did the calf turn to run but Crown dived and caught hold of its rear legs.

The calf struggled and bleated, and the cow went berserk. She charged toward her offspring and was brought up short by the rope. This time she crashed down but she was immediately back up and bucking and fighting to break free.

Crown had grabbed the calf's front legs, too, and was trying to lift it.

If Fargo had to guess, he'd say the calf wasn't more than two or three weeks old, and weighed somewhere between seventy and a hundred pounds. That wasn't a lot but the calf was doing all it could to resist being taken.

Rafer Crown performed a feat Fargo had seen cowboys use.

With a wrench on the calf's legs, he upended it onto its back. Before the calf could try to kick free, he swung in a circle, and then another, raising the calf higher with each swing. At the apex of his second turn he took a long bound and swung the calf up and over his saddle as neatly as you please. Another bound, and Crown was in the saddle and holding the calf in place even as he hauled on his reins. "Got it!" he cried.

Momentarily paralyzed with fright, the calf didn't try to jump down.

They had to get a rope on it fast, though.

Fargo started toward Crown, thinking he'd have to pull the cow after him. But she came willingly, heading for the bay and her young one.

Fargo was pleased at how well it had gone—for about ten seconds.

That was when Glyn Richmond shouted, "Thunderhead is coming!"

39

Beckoning to Rafer Crown and Richmond, Fargo made for the right-hand canyon wall near the bend. He got there first and reined up.

Crown was careful not to get too close to the cow. The calf continued to lie docile over the saddle. Part of it had to do with the fact that Crown wasn't using his stirrups. He was sitting farther back on the saddle than he normally would and had one leg across the calf's rear legs and his other leg over the calf's front legs to hold it in place.

The cow—Fargo kept forgetting that her name was Mabel— was being docile, too, staring forlornly at her calf.

Glyn Richmond trotted up, saying, "What the hell are we doing? We should be riding for our lives."

"Right into Thunderhead?" Fargo said.

"Use your damn noggin," Crown said.

"This worked once," Fargo said. "It might work again."

"What worked?" Glyn asked. "What are you talking about?"

Fargo's explanation was nipped in the bud by the drumming of heavy hooves.

Around the bend flew Thunderhead. He didn't look to the right or left. His gaze was locked on the thicket, where he thought the cow and the calf were. Without slowing, he plunged into the trail to the center.

"Quick," Fargo said. "Before he discovers they're gone. Rafer, you have to lead."

Crown gigged his bay and headed down the canyon.

Without Fargo having to do a thing, Mabel headed after him.

"I think I get what you're up to," Glyn said. "She'll follow us anywhere so long as we have the calf. And Thunderhead will follow her."

"We hope," Fargo said. Thunderhead might do as he had done on the long trek from Texas, or he might try to kill them.

They hurried, each of them casting repeated glances back.

When they were almost to the canyon mouth, Glyn looked back once more and said, "Dear God. I hope this plan of yours works or we're dead."

Thunderhead was at the bend, staring after them. His head was high and he was turning it from side to side and sniffing.

"Do we stop and wait to see what he'll do?" Crown called.

"We keep going," Fargo said. To Glyn he said, "Go fetch your sister and Dirk Peters. Follow after us but stay a ways back."

"In case of the bull?"

"In case of the bull."

Glyn nodded, and as soon as they were out of the canyon, he reined to the north and galloped off.

Crown pointed the bay in the general direction of the far-off ranch. He still had his legs over the calf, which had twisted its head and was looking at its mother.

Fargo let Mabel move closer to Crown's bay, but not so close that she could gore it.

The familiar drumming of hooves to their rear made Crown look back. "Get set. Here he comes."

The moment of truth was upon them.

Fargo willed himself to stay calm as Thunderhead overtook them. He shifted in the saddle, his skin prickling as the bull moved past the Ovaro. Up close, the monster seemed even more gigantic.

Thunderhead didn't so much as glance at him. The bull had eyes only for Mabel. It came alongside her and slowed.

Crown had one hand on a pistol. "I'll be damned," he said. "It's working."

It appeared to be. Mabel was following the calf and Thunderhead was glued to her.

"Do you reckon he'll let us lead him all the way down?" Crown asked.

"Only one way to find out," Fargo said.

For over an hour they worked their way lower. They saw no sign of the surviving Blackfeet or any of the other bull hunters. Not even the three they were looking for.

Rafer Crown gave voice to Fargo's own question. "Where the

hell can they be? Dirk and those two should have been here by now. One of us should go look."

"We can't stop yet," Fargo said.

"The farther we get . . ." Crown didn't finish.

"I know."

It was another half an hour before they reached the tree line. As much as Fargo wanted to push on, he took a gamble. He told Crown to rein up. When Crown complied, Mabel stopped, and when she stopped, Thunderhead halted.

"I'll be damned," the bounty hunter said.

Now came the part that could result in either or both of them being gored.

Moving slowly so as not to agitate the bull, Fargo dismounted. He undid the rope from the saddle horn, stepped to a sizable spruce, and tied it off, leaving a good two feet at the end lying on the ground.

Mabel had eyes only for her calf but Thunderhead watched everything Fargo did.

"Easy does it," Crown said.

Drawing the Arkansas toothpick, Fargo cut off the two feet of rope and replaced the toothpick. He moved wide around the bull and the cow and approached the bay.

The calf uttered a bleat of fear.

Instantly, Fargo stopped. All it would take was for the cow to show alarm and Thunderhead might charge.

Crown commenced stroking the calf's neck and speaking softly, saying, "Stupid damn calf."

When Mabel didn't act up, Fargo stepped to the bay and quickly fashioned a hobble that he slipped over the calf's front legs.

"Good idea," Crown said.

Reaching up, Fargo slid both arms under the calf, and when Crown eased his legs off, he carefully lowered it. The calf thrashed but only until its hooves touched the ground.

Then it tried to bound to its mother but the hobble hampered it and it tripped and almost fell. Catching itself, it managed to reach her side.

Thunderhead didn't move, didn't so much as twitch an ear. All he did was stare.

"That bull is spooky," Crown said.

Returning to the Ovaro, Fargo gripped the reins and led the stallion back a dozen yards.

Crown reined around the bovine family and joined him.

Letting out a sigh of relief, he said, "So far, so good."

"One of us has to stay with them and the other has to go see what's keeping the others," Fargo said.

"I don't mind staying. I don't like that Glyn Richmond much."

"I noticed."

"He's one of those as thinks he knows it all. They raise my hackles."

Fargo squinted at the sun. "I should be back before sundown."

"If nothing has happened."

"Don't jinx it," Fargo said, grinning.

"Jinx, hell," the bounty hunter said. "Whoever is killing us bull hunters is still out there. You and the others will be lucky to make it back alive."

40

The hell of it was, Rafer Crown was right.

Fargo rode alertly. He was concerned for Dirk Peters and Aramone. Glyn, he didn't give a damn about.

He was also concerned for Crown. So far Thunderhead had behaved but it wouldn't take much to trigger the bull's rage. By rights two or three of them should be watching over the longhorn at all times. If Crown wasn't careful, he could wind up like those gored Blackfeet.

It further reinforced Fargo's decision that this was the first and last bull bounty he'd ever go after.

He made a beeline for the firs where he'd left the others. Forty-five minutes of hard riding and he was there.

He was surprised to see gray tendrils rising from the trees. They must still be there.

One of them was.

Dirk Peters lay where Fargo had last seen him. His wound had been bandaged and there was a tin cup near his outstretched good arm. His throat had been cut from ear to ear and his neck and buckskin shirt were scarlet with dried blood. His eyes were wide in surprise.

It told Fargo that whoever killed him either snuck up on him, or it was someone Peters didn't suspect would try to harm him.

Alighting, Fargo palmed his Colt.

There was no sign of Aramone or her brother, and all the horses were gone.

The fire had burned almost out, so they had been gone a while.

Fargo roved for sign. He found no footprints other than those of Peters and the Richmonds. A cold feeling came over him, as of an icy wind on a winter's day.

Hoofprints showed that the Richmonds had headed north.

That was strange. The ranch was to the east. The canyon where Thunderhead and his family had hid was to the south.

Why go north?

Something else was strange.

Aramone and Glyn rode so close together, their animals were practically brushing one another. They might have done that for a while to talk but they had gone on doing it for over a mile. It made Fargo think of how cavalry troopers would bunch up in a column when hostiles threatened.

It also made him wonder if the Blackfeet were still around. Thunderhead had chased them off but they might have returned.

"Damn this bull business, anyhow," he grumbled.

Presently the tracks swung to the east and the spacing and depth revealed that the Richmonds had brought their horses to a trot.

Fargo began to wonder if maybe the pair had killed Peters and were circling to overtake Crown and him.

The Richmonds might intend to get ahead of them and wait in ambush. They could pick Crown and him off and have the bull and his family to themselves, and the bounty once they reached the Tyler spread.

It puzzled Fargo, though, that they continued to ride so close together. And after only a quarter of a mile they had slowed to a walk again.

It made no damn sense.

When he heard voices, he drew rein. They came to him on the upslope wind from somewhere close by. Sliding down, he held the reins and stalked forward.

Under different circumstances the mountain meadow rife with wildflowers would be picturesque. Now Fargo only had eyes for the pair seated by the fire they had just kindled.

Beyond were the horses, picketed.

Fargo couldn't get over how brazen they were about it. It fueled his anger. They were huddled together, talking. Their backs were to him but now and then Glyn would look sharply around.

The next time, as soon as Glyn lowered his head, Fargo walked into the open with his Colt level at his waist. He didn't try to sneak up on them. He simply walked over. When one of his spurs jingled, they leaped to their feet and spun.

"Skye!" Aramone happily exclaimed.

"Are we glad to see you," Glyn said, almost sounding sincere.

Fargo pointed his Colt and thumbed back the hammer. "I liked Dirk Peters."

"What?" Glyn said.

"No," Aramone said. "You don't think we did it?"

"Yours are the only tracks."

"It wasn't us," Glyn said.

"Honest it wasn't," Aramone echoed.

"Put your pistols on the ground," Fargo said. He looked at Aramone. "Both of you."

"Damn you," Glyn bristled. "How many times must we say it wasn't us? Someone snuck up and killed Peters when we weren't looking."

"That's right," Aramone said, bobbing her chin. "We were getting the horses ready and heard Dirk make funny sounds and turned, and there he was with his throat slit."

"I'd like to believe you," Fargo said. He wagged his Colt. "But drop your guns anyway."

"You pigheaded frontiersman," Glyn said. "Do you think we would lie?"

"You would," Fargo said bluntly. "I thought better of your sister."

"Oh, Skye," Aramone said. "It's not what you think."

"For the last time," Fargo said. "Your guns."

They looked at each other and Aramone said, "Let's do as he wants. Please. For me."

"Hell," Glyn said.

"We have to make him see the truth."

"And what about the killer?" Glyn said. "What about whoever has been stalking us?"

"No one has been stalking you," Fargo said. "I'd have seen the sign."

"I'm telling you someone is," Glyn said. "We heard a horse once or twice."

"Over that way," Aramone said, pointing to the north.

Fargo trained his Colt on Glyn's face. "I'll count to three."

Aramone opened her riding jacket and set down her pistol. "Please, brother."

Glyn's jaw was twitching and his fists were clenched. "I won't forget you for this."

"You won't have to if you're dead."

With an angry jerk, Glyn opened his own jacket, gripped his short-barreled Colt with two fingers, yanked it from his shoulder holster, and let it fall. "Happy now, you son of a bitch?"

"It's a start," Fargo said.

41

Fargo had Aramone take a rope from their packhorse and bind her brother's wrists and ankles. Glyn glared at her and as she was tying the last knot he swore and said, "You have just made the worst mistake of our lives."

"I can get him to see the truth," she replied. "Trust me."

"You're forgetting whoever is out there," Glyn said. "And now I'm helpless."

Fargo told Aramone to lie on her belly with her hands behind her back.

"You're tying me too?"

"I am," Fargo said.

"After how friendly I've been?"

"Lie down," Fargo said gruffly.

Reluctantly, she obeyed.

Fargo straddled her legs and gripped her left wrist and felt something under her long sleeve. "What's this?"

He slid the sleeve up, revealing a wrist sheath with a knife.

"You told us to drop our guns. You said nothing about dropping our knives."

"Dirk had his throat slit."

"It wasn't with mine, I assure you."

The blade didn't have so much as a spot of dried blood but that could be because she'd wiped it clean. Fargo tossed it aside and bound her wrists.

"My brother's right, you know. You're making a terrible mistake."

"My mistake," Fargo said, "was in thinking this bounty would be easy." He rolled her over, then went to the fire and touched the coffeepot.

"I just hope whoever has been picking us off decides to kill you next," Glyn said.

"Give it a rest." Fargo was tired of the whole business.

"I know it looks bad but I'd like you to hear me out," Aramone said. "We were talking it over and we've decided we can't do this ourselves. You were right all along. We're out of our element. We don't mind helping out and sharing the bounty."

"Generous of you," Fargo said, "now that Peters is dead and your share will be bigger."

"Is that what you suspect? That we murdered him for the money?"

"It's a possibility." Fargo looked over. "Do yourself a favor. Don't talk. Don't say a single word."

Aramone went to respond but didn't and slumped as if in despair.

"That goes double for you," Fargo warned when Glyn rose on an elbow.

Fargo was eager for some coffee. He needed to drink and think. He rose to get his tin cup and saw that the Ovaro had its head up and ears pricked and was staring into the woods to the north.

Fargo did the same. He saw nothing to account for it but a sensation came over him, one he'd experienced before, always when unseen eyes were on him. His hand drifted to his Colt.

"What?" Aramone said.

Fargo shook his head. He tried to tell himself it was nerves but he was hardly the skittish sort. And the Ovaro was still staring. Something, or someone, *was* out there.

"Untie us," Glyn whispered.

"No."

"If we're killed it will be on your shoulders."

"I told you to shut up."

Fargo moved to the trees. He crouched and let time go by but the forest stayed still. Too still. He didn't hear any birds or squirrels.

He glanced at the Richmonds. They were staring into the woods, too, their worry obvious. Could it be he had jumped to the wrong conclusion?

Off in the trees a twig snapped and he caught a fleeting glimpse of *something*.

Fargo flattened. It could be an animal but every instinct he had said different.

Twisting, he crawled to where the dagger and the six-shooters lay.

A few slashes and Aramone was free. "Thank you," she said.

"You've finally come to your senses," Glyn spat.

Fargo shoved the dagger at Aramone. "Stay down until I get back."

"Where are you going?"

"Where do you think?"

"We'll go with you."

"Like hell we will," Glyn said.

Fargo had no more time to waste. He crawled to the trees and slipped in among them and prayed he wouldn't regret what he'd just done.

42

Fargo snaked toward where he had glimpsed movement. His Colt was out and cocked. He avoided a boulder, slipped up and over a log. Pausing to listen, he heard the faintest of metallic clicks.

Fargo rolled just as a rifle cracked. The slug missed his ear by a whisker's-width. Rising on his elbows, he banged off a shot.

Other rifles blasted but not at him and were answered by Glyn's short-barreled Colt.

Aramone Richmond cried out.

Fargo fired at a muzzle flash and had to hunt cover as two rifles were turned on him. Lead clipped a pine above him and needles rained.

Glyn Richmond's short-barreled Colt boomed twice.

Fargo waited for the rifles to fire again but they didn't. He rose partway, seeking a target. There was none. The woods had gone unnaturally quiet again.

Then a horse nickered and hooves drummed.

Bursting into motion, Fargo raced after it. He might not get a shot but maybe he could see who it was.

Other hooves pounded, off to his right.

The thick timber forced Fargo to weave and dodge. It slowed him, and although he ran until his lungs ached, the hoofbeats faded.

The shooters had escaped.

Fargo swore lustily. Once again he'd been thwarted through no fault of his own. He stood listening for a while, until he was satisfied they were gone.

Reloading as he went, Fargo returned to the Richmonds.

Aramone was on her knees, cradling her brother's bloody head in her lap. She was quietly weeping, tears streaming down her cheeks.

Fargo didn't need to ask what had happened. A hole in Glyn Richmond's temple sufficed. He put his hand on Aramone's shoulder and gently squeezed.

She didn't look up, didn't acknowledge him at all. She went on crying, her sorrow was so overwhelming.

Fargo went to the Ovaro and shucked the Henry from the scabbard on the off chance the would-be assassins tried again.

The sun dipped low over the stark peaks to the west, and Aramone finally wept herself dry. She sniffled and wiped at her nose with a sleeve and said forlornly, "They killed him."

"Did you see who it was?" Fargo was anxious to learn.

Aramone shook her head. "There were three, I think. That's all I could tell." She did more sniffling. "We'd heard shots and he jumped at me and made me lie flat and drew his Colt, and the next one hit him in the head."

"That was you firing back?"

Aramone nodded. "I grabbed Glyn's pistol. I doubt I hit anyone. I never saw them. It was like they were ghosts."

"Ghosts don't blow holes in people," Fargo declared, and was sorry he'd said it when she clutched her brother's shirt and broke into fresh tears.

It would be a while before she stopped.

Fargo climbed on the Ovaro and rode in a wide half circle. There had to be footprints. Scuff marks. Some sign of their attackers. But half an hour of searching proved fruitless.

His frustration knew no bounds.

Returning, he saw that the fire had burned out. He rekindled the embers.

Aramone was hunched over with her cheek on her brother's chest and her eyes closed. Fargo figured she had drifted off but then he saw she was staring at him.

"Why?" she asked in sheer misery.

"It has to be the bounty," Fargo said.

Slowly sitting up, she absently ran a hand over her hair. "It wasn't the Blackfeet?"

"That's the one thing I'm sure of."

Aramone traced Glyn's jaw with a fingertip. "You might not have liked him but he was a good brother."

"If you say so."

"He looked after me after our parents died. It was my idea to go into the bounty business. Escaped slaves, mostly, to start. There's good money in that."

Fargo was aware that plantation owners often placed high bounties. But he never had liked the notion of one man being another's property.

"They rarely raise a fuss when you catch them. They're too afraid of being hung."

"Who wouldn't be?" Fargo said, but she didn't seem to hear him.

"We went after escaped convicts now and then but the bounties were never very much. Outlaws. What have you." Aramone sucked in a deep breath and more tears trickled. "All the dangerous people my brother and I caught over the past few years, and he meets his end hunting a goddamned cow."

"Thunderhead is a bull."

"Same thing."

No, it wasn't, but Fargo let it drop. "You can have your brother's share once we get the money."

Aramone brightened slightly. "That's awful nice of you. But your bounty hunter friend might not go for the idea."

"It won't hurt to ask him."

"God," she said sorrowfully. "It just hit me. I have to start a whole new life. What will do I? I'm not much of a cook and I can't sew worth a lick. All I know how to do is hunt bounties."

Fargo was worried about something else. "Do you want your brother buried?"

"What kind of question is that? Do you think I want the coyotes and buzzards tearing at him? Why would you even ask?"

"Because whoever took those shots at us and killed your brother might be going after Crown and Thunderhead."

Aramone considered that. "I need my share of the bounty now more than ever. Let's bury Glyn, but it needn't be deep."

So much for sisterly love, Fargo thought.

"Do you think we'll have a chance to get even with the killers?" she asked.

"As sure as the sun rises and sets," Fargo said.

"What makes you say that?"

"They have to kill us to get their hands on the bull."

"Oh," Aramone said.

43

They set the extra horses free in the meadow. After Thunderhead was delivered, Fargo would have Jim Tyler send a cowhand for them.

They rode as if Rafer Crown's life depended on it.

Fargo was loath to push the Ovaro after having ridden so hard the past couple of days. Thank God for the stallion's exceptional stamina.

Aramone grimly rode in his wake, her hair flying in the wind.

Presently the sun was almost gone, and they'd only descended a third of the way. Once it set, Fargo would have no choice but to go slower. He wouldn't risk losing the stallion to a misstep in the dark.

As it turned out, he had to slow sooner when Aramone shouted, "Hold up! Please!"

"What is it?" Fargo impatiently asked once they had drawn rein.

"I can't keep up with you. I'm sorry. I'm not as good a rider. I've almost ridden into trees twice now. Go on without me if you have to."

Fargo wasn't about to leave her at the mercy of the mystery killers and whatever wild beasts happened along.

"We go together."

"I can't keep up, I tell you."

"Then we go slower."

Fargo constantly sought the glow of a campfire. Either Crown hadn't kindled a fire, which was unlikely, or the bounty hunter wisely kindled his fire where it couldn't be seen.

When the terrain permitted, Aramone rode at his side.

It was just Fargo's luck that her loss had made her gabby.

"It hasn't been a couple of hours and I miss my brother terribly. Whoever shot him has to pay."

"Goes without saying," Fargo said.

"I've never been out for revenge before. It's not in my nature to kill."

"All those bounties you collected, you took them alive?"

"We always tried to. Glyn would have shot a few more than he actually did but I usually talked him out of it."

"Why are you telling me this?"

"I've had time to think as we rode," Aramone said, "and I don't know if I can kill them without cause."

"What the hell do you call shooting your brother?"

"I know, I know. I only meant I might not have it in me to walk up to someone and pull a gun and shoot them dead."

"They'd do it to you."

"Maybe so. But I'm the one who has to live with my conscience, afterward." Aramone peered at him in the dark. "Doesn't it ever bother you?"

"Now and then."

"But you do it anyway?"

"When I have to."

"I wish I had your courage."

"All you need," Fargo said, "is the will." He might have gone on but just then she pointed.

"Look there!"

A dancing finger of orange wasn't more than half a mile off, Fargo reckoned.

"Is it Crown, do you think?"

"We'll soon find out."

"If we can see his fire," Aramone mentioned, "so can anyone."

Fargo rode faster.

He was startled to find that the fire was right out in the open, on a broad grassy bench with a lone tree in the middle. Mabel was tied to it. She was resting, the calf next to her. A few yards away lay Thunderhead, peacefully chewing.

"Where's the bounty hunter?" Aramone asked.

Fargo had no idea. Neither Rafer Crown nor Crown's horse were anywhere to be seen. He threw caution aside and rode toward the fire.

Thunderhead showed no alarm whatsoever. Mabel raised her droopy eyelids and went back to dozing. The calf was asleep.

Drawing rein, Fargo looked around. "What the hell?"

"Where can he have got to?" Aramone said.

From out of the tall pine drifted a voice. "Look up and I'll spit in your face. That should give you a clue."

Craning his neck, Fargo curled his lips in a smile. "You clever son of a bitch."

"I have my moments," Crown said.

Limbs moved and rustled and a dark silhouette clambered down. Crouching on a bottom limb, Rafer Crown grinned. He had a Spencer rifle in his left hand.

Fargo remembered seeing the stock jutting from Crown's saddle scabbard but the bounty hunter hadn't relied on it until now.

"Anyone wants the bull, they could come and get him," Crown said with a grin.

"And you'd pick them off as easy as you please," Aramone said. "You up that tree, and they have all this open ground to cover."

"You learn quick, gal," Crown complimented her.

"I'm a full-grown woman," Aramone replied, "or haven't you noticed?"

"A man would have to be half dead not to."

"If you two are done," Fargo interrupted, "where's your horse?"

"Hid over in the woods," Crown said.

"What if someone finds him," Fargo said. "The Blackfeet, for instance."

"He'll raise a hell of a fuss," Crown said, his grin widening. "He's a devil with anyone but me." Gripping the limb, he nimbly swung down and landed lightly on the balls of his boots.

"What made you think of this?" Aramone asked with a nod at the fire and the tree.

"I hunt men for a living," Crown said. "Men who would as soon see me dead. Staying one step ahead of them is how I stay alive." His eyes narrowed. "Where's your brother and that chatterbox Peters?"

"Gone," Fargo said.

"Both?"

"Both," Aramone confirmed sadly.

"Damn. I liked Dirk. He was growing on me. And I'm right sorry about your brother."

Aramone coughed.

"Who's to blame?" Crown asked.

"I honestly don't know," Fargo admitted. "I couldn't find any tracks."

"How are they outsmarting us?" Crown asked.

"If I knew the how," Fargo answered, "they wouldn't be."

"Whoever they are, they almost had us, too," Aramone said. "The bastards shot at us from ambush."

Crown looked at the longhorn bull. "All these deaths. That farmer. That old gal. The others we found, and who knows how many we didn't. And now Dirk and your brother." He paused. "Is this critter worth all those lives?"

"No," Aramone said.

"The important thing," Fargo said, "is to find out who's been taking them and take theirs."

"Amen to that," Rafer Crown said.

44

They spent a remarkably peaceful night.

Crown climbed back up into the pine and spent another three hours and then it was Fargo's turn. He chose a vantage high up where he could see anyone who tried to get close.

Fargo stayed up the tree until the first rays of the sun lit the eastern sky.

Mabel stirred, and the calf woke and wanted a turn at her teats.

As for Thunderhead, he was a whole new bull. Gone was the belligerence, the anger. He acted as tame and friendly as the calf.

It was a mystery why the longhorn had been so set to gore them to keep them from the canyon, but now that they had a rope over Mabel and were leading her off, he came along as peacefully as anything.

What was that saying? Fargo reflected as he took a swallow of his first coffee of the day. Be thankful for small blessings?

Aramone awakened, fussed with her clothes, and poured a cup of her own. Or so Fargo thought until she stepped over to where Crown lay on his side with his arm for a pillow and lightly touched his shoulder.

At the contact, the bounty hunter sat bolt upright, his hands sweeping to his six-shooters. He looked all around and said, "What is it? Are they out there?"

"I brought you breakfast," Aramone said, smiling and holding out the cup.

"You did what?"

"They call it coffee," she joked.

His brow knit, Crown accepted the cup. "I'm obliged, ma'am."

"Call me Aramone," she said. "All my friends do." She turned and moved back to the fire, her hips swaying a little more than they usually did.

Crown's expression almost made Fargo laugh. The bounty hunter might be a terror when it came to tracking wanted men but he had a lot to learn about females.

To tease Aramone, Fargo said, "How about eggs and bacon while you're at it?"

"Would that I could," she replied. "And how dare you mention food. I'm half starved."

"We'll eat a good meal tonight," Crown said, "if I have to make it myself."

"I'd be ever so grateful," Aramone said sweetly.

Fargo couldn't be sure but he thought the bounty hunter's cheek grew slightly red. He intruded on their romance by remarking, "I figure it'll take us three to four days to reach the ranch."

"We can make it sooner if I throw the calf over my horse," Crown said.

"Why agitate the cow if we don't have to?" Fargo said. "It might rile Thunderhead and we don't want that."

"No, we sure as hell don't," Crown agreed.

"Three or four days," Aramone repeated, "with whoever is out there slinking after us every step of the way."

Crown squinted at the rising sun, pulled his hat brim lower, and gnawed on his bottom lip. "The way I see it, they won't hit us when we're close to the ranch. Too great a chance of them being seen."

"So it will likely be today or the next," Aramone said.

"The farther out, the better for them," Crown said.

"You expect them to try this very day?"

"I do," Crown told her.

So did Fargo. They must be constantly on their guard. "It might be smart to have an outrider."

"I was thinking the same thing," Rafer Crown said.

"A what?" Aramone asked. "That's a new one on me."

Crown answered before Fargo could. "One of us shadows the other two and our little family of beeves. The idea is that he spots the killers before they commence the killing, and blows them to hell."

"What if the killers spot him?"

"There's that," Crown said.

"Which of you will it be?"

"Him," Crown said.

Fargo had thought the bounty hunter might want to. Then he

remembered Aramone's swaying hips and raised his tin cup to cover his grin.

"If you're sure," Aramone said, sounding relieved.

"I am," Crown said. "I should stay with the"—he caught himself—"longhorns."

Fargo made a show of gazing about them. "It's too bad roses don't grow in the Rockies."

"Go to hell," Crown said.

"What?" Aramone said. "What was that about roses?"

Crown distracted her by saying, "Even with him out there, we have to take precautions. I'll lead the cow and you'll ride close to the bull."

"Why don't I lead Mabel?" Aramone asked. "Doesn't that make more sense?"

"They won't shoot Thunderhead. He's worthless to them dead. Odds are they won't risk hitting him by shooting at you if you're near him."

"Oh," Aramone said. "You want to protect me."

This time Fargo was certain. The bounty hunter flushed.

"Don't make more of it than there is," Crown said gruffly.

"I'm not," Aramone said in that sweet way she had.

Fargo drained his cup and stood. "Yes, sir. A rose and a violin would come in handy right about now." Before the bounty hunter could respond, he said, "Let's fetch your horse and move out." He added, "And for once, let's hope luck is on our side."

"Yes," Aramone said. "It would be nice to end the day alive."

45

Pins and needles, some called it. Being on edge every second of every minute. Never knowing when they'd be attacked. Having to stay razor-alert every moment.

The first couple of hours weren't so hard but after five or six Fargo had to work at it to not let his mind wander.

It didn't help that the day was as ordinary as any other. Birds warbled and hawks and eagles soared. Deer grazed and several elk retreated into cover. Now and then a butterfly flitted about.

It was so peaceful, it about put Fargo to sleep.

Thankfully, the longhorns behaved. Thunderhead plodded along behind Mabel and the calf as happily as a married man on his wife's leash.

Fargo was constantly on the go. He shadowed them to the north and then he'd cut their back trail or ride ahead a ways and shadow them to the south.

By the middle of the afternoon the Ovaro could use a rest and Fargo had to concentrate to stay sharp.

And still no sign of anyone out to do them harm.

By sundown Fargo was ready for a rest.

They'd descended a series of forested slopes to a verdant valley. Instead of following it to the east, Rafer Crown rode out to the center near a stand of aspens and stopped. He and Aramone climbed down and set about making camp.

Fargo broke from cover and joined them. To the west the sun was almost gone. The shadows were spreading and soon twilight would fall.

"So far, so good," Aramone said cheerfully as he rode up.

"It's only a matter of time," Fargo said as he wearily alighted.

Crown had loosened the cinch on his saddle and was about to

slide it off. "We'll tie the cow here and lie low in the aspens. Each of us at a different spot so between us we can see the whole valley."

"You think of everything," Aramone praised him.

"Here we go again," Fargo said.

"What?"

"If you bring up roses I will by-God shoot you," the bounty hunter said.

"Do we make a fire or not?" Aramone asked. "I could go with some coffee."

So could Fargo. "We'll make the fire out here and keep it burning most of the night."

"Whoever is after us will see it," Aramone observed.

"We want them to," Crown said. "So they try to sneak in for the bull and we blow out their wicks."

"I do so admire a man who knows what he is about," Aramone said.

Fargo could use a drink stronger than coffee. Better yet, a bottle.

Crown used a picket pin to stake Mabel so she wouldn't wander off. The calf took to her teats while Thunderhead stood gazing at them, looking for all the world like a proud father.

"Aren't they cute?" Aramone said.

Fargo thought of the warriors the bull had gored and the other men he'd killed. "Cute," he said.

They led their horses into the aspens and tied them, then gathered firewood and came back out and Crown started a fire.

By then the sun had relinquished the heavens to the brightening stars, and the lonesome wail of a wolf heralded the new night.

Fargo saw to the coffee himself. He noticed that Aramone sat near Rafer Crown and kept showing him what nice teeth she had.

"If they don't try tonight," the bounty hunter brought up, "it will be tomorrow."

"Do we do the same as today?" Aramone asked.

"Unless Fargo has an objection," Crown said, "I'm for it."

Fargo couldn't resist. "The two of you and Thunderhead and Mabel make such charming couples, I wouldn't want to break you up."

"Have I told you to go to hell lately?" Crown asked.

Fargo laughed.

"You men," Aramone said.

Fargo was amused by how she was throwing herself at the bounty hunter. He was even more amused that the bounty hunter didn't seem to mind. It proved the saying down in Texas that when a filly threw a loop, there was always someone ready to step into it.

He certainly wasn't. It would be a good many years, if ever, before he was ready to have his spurs trimmed. Married life was fine for most men but for him it would be the same as a cage.

"What do you plan to do with your share of the bounty?" Aramone asked Crown.

"I don't think about spending money until I have it in my poke."

"Wise," Aramone said. "Very wise."

"Anyone hear a violin?" Fargo said.

"A what?" Aramone said.

Crown glared.

"That reminds me," Fargo said. "Didn't you say something about cooking?"

Muttering, the bounty hunter got up and strode into the aspens.

"Is it me," Aramone said, "or are you poking fun at him?"

"Me?" Fargo said.

Crown came back with a pan and flour and something wrapped in a bundle. A canteen hung from a strap over his shoulder. "Biscuits and bacon should do us."

"We're having breakfast?" Fargo said.

"She and me are," Crown said. "One more jab out of you and you can go hungry."

Their banter had done wonders to ease the tension Fargo had been under all day. He was just starting to relax, and eased back onto his elbows.

"I must say," Aramone said, "this is a pleasant change after all the worrying I've been doing. Let's hope we have a nice, peaceful night."

"I'm afraid you won't," someone said, and Rance Hollister stepped into the firelight with his Sharps to his shoulder.

46

The Sharps was a single-shot but that shot was powerful enough to bring down a buffalo at a thousand yards. Or to blow a whole in a man the size of an apple. Which was why Fargo froze.

Rafer Crown didn't. He spun, his hands poised to draw, then saw that the Sharps's muzzle was pointed at Aramone Richmond.

"You're quick enough that you might get me," Rance said, "but not before I blow her to hell."

Fargo wanted to beat his head against a boulder for being so careless. He'd let down his guard for just a bit, and look.

As if Rance had read his thoughts, he smirked and said, "You made it plumb easy for us. Isn't that right, brothers?"

"It sure is," Kyler Hollister replied as he and Grizz came out of the stand. Kyler held his knife, Grizz his six-shooter.

"They're dumb as stumps," Grizz said, and guffawed.

Aramone was staring at the muzzle pointed at her face. "You're those Hollisters I've heard about."

"Good things, I hope?" Rance said, and his brothers chortled.

"We have that five thousand to collect," Kyler said.

"It was right nice of you and your man friends to bring the bull this far for us."

"Right nice," Grizz echoed.

"Where's that brother we know you have?" Rance asked Aramone. "And that Peters fella? How come they're not with you?"

"You don't know?" Aramone said in surprise.

"If I did, you dumb bitch, I wouldn't have asked."

"They're both dead," Aramone enlightened him. "After what Skye told me, I thought you three might have been to blame."

"It weren't us," Kyler said. "It must have been those Blackfeet."

"Lousy redskins," Grizz said.

"Now, now," Rance said. "They've done us a favor by whittlin' the odds. We should be grateful for their help."

"We should?" Grizz said.

"Not so grateful that we won't shoot them on sight."

"That's better. For a second there, I thought you were turnin' into an Injun lover."

"Not me, brother. You know me better. It's the three of us against the world."

It was then that the thought that had been gnawing at the back of Fargo's mind leaped out as clear as a cloudless day. "I'll be damned," he blurted.

"We all are," Rance Hollister said. "But that's neither here nor there. It's time to tend to business. So how about if you and the bounty hunter shed your hardware or I kill the lady."

"You aim to kill us whether we do or we don't," Rafer Crown said.

"Maybe so," Rance said, "but if you don't, this gal's pretty eyes and nose are splattered over the grass that much sooner."

"Don't listen to him," Aramone urged Crown. "Do what you must."

"I'll gamble with a lot of things but not your life," Rafer said. He undid his belt buckle and the Remington and the Smith & Wesson thumped to earth.

"Like takin' candy from a baby," Rance gloated, and focused on Fargo. "Your turn, scout. And don't forget your pigsticker."

Slowly sitting up, Fargo hiked at his pant leg. "There's something you should know."

"Oh?"

"You're not the only ones who will do anything for the bounty," Fargo said.

"Meanin' yourself? What can you do with your claws clipped?"

"Others besides me," Fargo said.

"Land sakes," Kyler said in mock fear. "I do believe he's tryin' to scare us."

"Stupid scout," Grizz said.

Rance took a step nearer. "That knife and that Colt, and we don't have all night."

Fargo set them to one side and raised his arms.

"Good. Real good." Rance chuckled and took a bound and drove the stock of his rifle into Rafer Crown's belly. Crown doubled over and staggered, and Aramone heaved to her feet to help him.

Kyler was faster. He flashed his knife to her throat and held it edgewise to her skin. "Another step and I cut you."

"This is fun," Grizz said.

Fargo wasn't surprised the Hollisters hadn't gunned them down. Not these three. They liked to play with their victims like cats played with mice.

Crown was on his knees, retching, his black hat practically brushing the ground.

"You're right, brother," Rance said to Grizz. "We'll have us a lot of laughs."

Despite the knife at her throat, Aramone spat, "You're animals, is what you are."

"And proud of it," Rance said.

Kyler said, "You don't get it, do you, gal? We don't live by no one's say-so but our own."

"That's right," Grizz declared.

"We do what we want, when we want, and everyone else be damned," Kyler gloated.

"That's right," Grizz said again, this time bobbing his bearded chin.

"We're curly wolves with the bark on," Kyler continued to crow, "and no one has ever got the better of us."

"That's right."

Kyler glared at Fargo. "Except once."

Grizz glared, too. "I owe you for the lickin' you gave me."

"That you do, brother," Rance said. "And pretty soon now you'll get to break every bone in his body."

"I can't wait."

"Please," Aramone said. "Just take the bull and go."

"Listen to you," Rance scoffed.

"What if . . . ?" Aramone stopped and looked at Rafer Crown, who had stopped retching but was still doubled over. "What if I offered myself to you if you'll leave my friends alone?"

"God Almighty, woman? Do you even have a brain? We're goin' to have our way with you anyway. And kill them, besides."

47

Fargo was glad the Hollisters were talkers. It gave him time to think, and increased the odds of them making a mistake.

They were about to make one now.

They were having so much fun mocking and threatening that Rance had let the barrel of his Sharps dip and Grizz had lowered his revolver to his side. Kyler still held his bone-handled knife but he was no longer pressing it to Aramone's throat.

Fargo was tempted to jump them but with Rafer Crown hurt it would be three to one. He tried another tack. "I have a question."

The brothers stopped smirking and Kyler said, "Listen to you. Polite as anything."

"Stupid scout," Grizz rumbled again.

"Ask it," Rance said.

"What are you fixing to do when the Blackfeet catch up to us?"

The mention of the terrors of the northern plains and mountains caused all three brothers to suddenly become serious.

"What's that?" Rance said.

"We've tangled with the war party twice," Fargo said, although a case could be made that Thunderhead did most of the tangling. "They killed Dirk Peters and this lady's brother," he outright lied, "and they're hard on our heels."

All three Hollisters glanced to the west.

"Like hell they are," Kyler scoffed, but he sounded uncertain.

Aramone gave Fargo a strange look and then must have caught on to what he was doing because she nodded and said, "That's right. Thunderhead scared them off the last time they came after us. They're afraid of him."

"He's a mighty big bull," Grizz said. "I'd be scared of him except I'm big too."

"Hush, you infant," Rance snapped. He stared hard at Fargo and then at Aramone as if trying to see through them.

"If that's true, why have you stopped for the night?"

"That's right," Kyler said. "Why ain't you runnin' like hell?"

"And leave them behind?" Fargo said, jerking his thumb at the longhorns. "After all the trouble we've gone to for that five thousand?"

Rance gazed to the west again. "We saw the war party once from far off but they didn't spot us."

"Seven or eight of them, weren't there?" Kyler said.

"I don't like Blackfeet," Grizz said. "They're mean."

Fargo fueled their worry by saying, "Everyone knows the Blackfeet don't travel at night. It's one of their superstitions." It was no such thing but he was banking on the Hollisters not knowing that. "Come daybreak, though, they'll be after us again."

"I've heard tell that most Injuns don't go anywhere after the sun goes down," Kyler said.

"Why are you tellin' us this?" Rance asked suspiciously.

"Because I'm not hankering to be scalped," Fargo answered.

"You damned idiot," Kyler said. "What makes you think you'll be breathin' come daylight?" He wagged his long knife and took a step toward Fargo.

"No," Rance said.

Kyler looked at him.

"The bull and the cow can only go so fast and they're what's important," Rance said. "No Thunderhead, no five thousand."

"So?" Kyler said.

"So we want to delay the redskins long enough for us to get away."

"How?"

Rance grinned a vicious grin. "I have me an idea. I'll cover them while you tie the scout and the bounty hunter. But no cuttin' on them, you hear? We want them in one piece."

"We do?"

"They're our gift to the Blackfeet."

Grizz's hairy face contorted in confusion. "They're what now?"

Kyler chuckled. "I get it, big brother. That's smart. Real smart." Still chuckling, he headed off into the darkness. "I'll fetch our horses and our rope."

Rance raised his Sharps and centered it on Fargo. "Thanks for the warnin'."

"I didn't mean it to be," Fargo played his part.

Rafer Crown wiped his mouth with his sleeve and slowly sat up. He'd caught on to Fargo's ruse and said, "You shouldn't have told them about the Blackfeet."

"Hush, you," Rance said. "It was right kind of him." And he laughed.

"I don't savvy any of this," Grizz said.

"It's simple, brother," Rance said. "There's a war party after these three."

"There is?"

"And if the Injuns catch up with the scout and the bounty hunter, here, guess what."

The lines in Grizz's brow deepened. "You know I'm not good at thinkin'."

"You think good enough to know what the Blackfeet do to whites they catch."

"They torture and kill them."

"Exactly. And they take a while at it, don't they?"

"So I've heard."

"Then if we leave the scout and the bounty hunter for them to find, they'll be at it a good long while. Givin' us time to slip clean away."

"That's smart, Rance. That's more than smart. What's that word? It's brilliant."

"Brotherly love," Fargo said.

Rance stopped smirking. "Insult us again and I'll splatter your innards. The bounty man will be enough to slow them a spell."

"What about me?" Aramone asked.

"What about you?"

"How do I fit into this plan of yours?"

Rance ogled her and licked his lips. "You fit right fine. We're takin' you with us."

"We are?" Grizz said.

"Wouldn't you like a poke?"

Grizz looked at her with lust in his eyes. "I'd like four or five."

"Now you know why."

"You think of everything, Rance," Grizz complimented him.

"One of us has to."

Fargo's ruse had bought him and the others some time.

But they were still in deadly peril, Aramone most of all.

He was under no illusions about what the Hollisters would do to her once they'd had their fun.

"Yes, sir," Rance was saying. "This has worked out real nice. And all because you warned me about the redskins."

"Go to hell," Fargo said.

"You'll be there long before me. I'll look you up when my time comes."

Grizz laughed.

"Yes, sir," Rance said. "The Blackfeet carve on you and him. Her, we rape. And then we get five thousand dollars for the bull. Life doesn't get any better."

48

"You and your brainstorms," Rafer Crown said when the sun was a couple of hours high in the sky.

Fargo didn't blame him for being angry. Here they were, each tied between different trees. "We're alive, aren't we?"

"Don't get me wrong. I'm glad your trick worked. But they have *her.*"

Fargo couldn't stop thinking about that, either. He liked Aramone. He only hoped the Hollisters would spend most of the day pushing hard to the east to escape the Blackfeet who weren't after them, and not lay a hand on her until nightfall. "How are you coming at getting free?"

"I can barely feel my arms and legs."

Fargo was the same. Kyler Hollister had taken particular delight in making the ropes as tight as he could.

"I'm bleeding down both arms. Not a lot, but still."

"Keep working at it."

"What in hell do you think I'm doing?"

The Hollisters had picked tall pines at the east end of the valley. When Crown asked why they were being tied between the trees rather than to the trunk, Rance replied that it would be easier for the Blackfeet to spot them.

"They can't torture you if they can't find you."

"And they do love to cut on us white folks," Kyler had added.

Grizz simply chuckled.

Despite working his wrists back and forth for the past two hours, all Fargo had to show for it was stripped flesh and pain and trickles of blood.

"We have to get free soon or they'll get too far ahead," Crown said.

"They can only go as fast as Mabel."

"Is that supposed to give me hope? They have horses and we'll be on foot."

Fargo twisted both wrists, or tried to. His agony doubled. To take his mind off it he remarked, "She's a fine lady, that Aramone."

"She sure is," Crown agreed with evident feeling.

"And she's a bounty hunter, besides."

"That too," Crown said, and lowered his voice as if he was afraid someone would overhear. "She's offered to work with me. With her brother gone, she's on her own, and collecting bounties will be a lot harder."

"With you as her partner, I'd say the two of you would do right fine."

"That's what she said."

Fargo couldn't help but reflect that when it came to throwing loops, women were more devious than men could ever be.

"We have to save her," Crown said. "We can't let those sons of bitches have their way."

"No, we can't."

"Just so you know," Crown said, "I'm killing all three of them."

"Only if I don't get to them first."

"That they'd abuse a fine gal like her is—" Crown suddenly stopped and jerked his head up and stared down the valley. "Tell me I'm seeing things."

Fargo looked and felt the blood in his veins turn to ice.

A grizzly had come out of the trees at the far end.

"If he catches wind of us, he's liable to eat us alive," Crown said.

"Maybe he won't," Fargo said. "Maybe he'll go elsewhere."

As if to prove how wrong he was, the grizzly started up the valley, looking for all the world as if he were out for a midmorning stroll.

Fargo wrenched at the ropes and set his skin to bleeding again.

Rafer Crown was doing the same in a near frenzy.

Fargo tugged and twisted, never once taking his eyes off the bear. He could think of few more horrible fates than being eaten alive.

Crown, too, was jerking and straining. "I refuse to goddamn die this way."

Fargo noticed some slack in the rope around his right wrist. He strained harder while working his wrist back and forth.

"Goddamn it," Crown fumed. "Goddamn it. Goddamn it. God-damn it."

"You'd better hope the Almighty's not listening."

Crown stopped for a moment to say, "How in hell can you josh at a time like this?"

"It beats crying."

They renewed their efforts. The grizzly was still hundreds of yards away and hadn't spotted them yet but was slowly coming in their direction.

"Look at the size of that thing," Crown said.

Fargo was intent on his right wrist. It was smeared with blood and slick enough that he could almost pull it loose. Twisting his wrist back and forth, he tried harder. Suddenly his hand was free.

"One down," he crowed, and attacked the knots in the rope around his left wrist. Prying and tugging, he loosened first one and then another. His fingers hurt like hell and he started to bleed from under a nail but he didn't stop. Not with their lives at stake.

He was so engrossed in freeing his left arm that he didn't pay attention to the bear.

Then Crown said, "Hell in a basket. We're in for it now."

Fargo looked up.

The grizzly had seen them.

49

Fargo redoubled his efforts to free his left arm. The rope had loosened but not enough that he could slide his hand from the loop.

"Look!" Crown exclaimed.

The grizzly had risen onto its hind legs and was staring fixedly at them.

"The size of him," Crown said in awe.

It was the teeth and claws that worried Fargo. One bite of those massive jaws and the bear could crush his skull like an eggshell. Or one swipe of those huge paws could open him like a gutted fish.

"What's he doing?"

The grizzly was tilting its head from side to side, its muzzle raised high.

"Trying to catch our scent," Fargo guessed. "He doesn't know what to make of us."

"And when he does?"

With a wrench that tore an inch of skin from his forearm, Fargo freed his other wrist. Quickly bending, he attacked the knots in the rope that held his right leg to the pine.

"I don't have much to do with bears," the bounty hunter said as he struggled mightily to break free. "I hunt men."

The bounty hunter was anxious, and Fargo didn't blame him. Facing a man in a gunfight was one thing. Facing the prospect of being clawed to ribbons was another.

"He's made up his mind."

Fargo looked up again.

The grizzly had dropped onto all fours and was lumbering toward them, sniffing as it came.

Suddenly Fargo's right leg was free. He turned to the knots on his left, pressing his nails so hard, it was a wonder they didn't break.

"Damn, damn, damn," Crown said as he continued to fling himself against his ropes.

The grizzly came on faster, as if the sight of the bounty hunter's struggles had triggered a reflex that here was meat for the eating.

The knots on Fargo's left leg were tight as hell. He pried and pried.

Crown was practically beside himself, struggling as if he'd gone berserk.

Twenty yards out, the grizzly stopped. With its enormous bulk, a mouth lined with inches-long teeth, and claws that could shred flesh as if it were paper, his kind were the undisputed lords of the Rockies. Or had been, until the coming of the white man with his guns. They'd roamed where they pleased, killing what and who they pleased.

Based on its bulk, this one looked to weigh close to seven hundred pounds.

Fargo always gave silver-tips a wide berth when he could. They were too deadly to tempt fate. The only other animal that came close to being as formidable was a riled buffalo.

The last knot loosened and he quickly tore the rope off and cast it away.

His movements had drawn the attention of the bear.

Fargo had seldom felt so helpless. He had no rifle, no revolver, no knife.

Rafer Crown let out a grunt. He'd finally freed his left arm and immediately went to work trying to free the other.

Fargo took a step to help him and the grizzly growled. Taking a gamble, he raising his pain-racked arms and waved them back and forth. "Go away! Do you hear me? Get the hell out of here!"

Sometimes that worked.

This time it didn't.

All the grizzly did was stare and sniff.

Crown was working furiously at the knots on his right wrist.

Fargo cast about for something to use as a weapon. A downed limb, a rock, anything. Not that either would do him much good. A grizzly was a living mountain of muscle and bone. Nothing short of a shot to the brain or the heart would bring one down.

"Come undone, damn you," Crown railed at a knot.

The griz growled.

Fargo saw a fallen branch. It wasn't thick or very long but the broken end came to a jagged point. Darting over, he picked it up and hefted it. As makeshift spears went, it was pitiful. But it was all he had.

"Fargo!" Crown cried.

Sniffing noisily, the bear was coming toward them.

Fargo moved in front of the bounty hunter and set himself.

"What do you think you're doing?"

"Protecting you."

"Like hell you are. Run for it. I'll try to keep him occupied and you go save her."

"No."

"Damn it," Crown fumed. "She matters more than me."

Fargo gripped the branch in both hands with the jagged end toward the bear. If he could jab it in the eyes. If he could blind it. Or maybe if he could strike hard enough in the throat. If, if, if.

"We can't let them do that to her," Crown said. "As a favor to me, go."

"No."

"They'll *rape* her."

"I know."

"You are one coldhearted son of a bitch."

Fargo was focused on the griz. It had stopped again, apparently because it was puzzled by the bounty hunter's outburst. He raised his makeshift spear, ready to thrust.

"Anytime you want to get loose, be my guest."

Crown went into a frenzy, tugging and yanking and all the while heaping invective on Fargo and the Hollisters and the bear. He used every cuss word Fargo ever heard and some Fargo hadn't. Finally he subsided and hung by his one arm, spent and defeated.

That was when the grizzly took another loud sniff, wheeled on its hind legs, and ponderously strolled off to the south.

"I'll be damned," Fargo said.

"Thank God," Crown said. "Now can we get to killing those Hollisters?"

50

It was said that an Apache could run seventy miles in a single day.

Fargo wasn't an Apache but he was a good runner. He'd taken part in a footrace once against some of the best runners in the country and a few from overseas and proven he could hold his own.

He ran now as he had run then, with a tireless stride that ate up the miles.

Rafer Crown wasn't an Apache, either. He was no Fargo, as well. He was used to getting around on horseback. When he wasn't riding, he walked. He hardly ever ran. Only the fact that he had more muscle on him than most let him keep up.

For two miles.

That was when Crown stopped and bent over with his hands on his knees. Wheezing and sputtering, he gasped, "You go on. I can't take another step."

"I'll wait."

"Think of Aramone."

"I am. There are three of them and one of me."

Crown spat and did more wheezing. "I'm acting like a damned baby, huh?"

"Let's just say I see diapers in your future."

Crown laughed and had to stop to gasp and groan. "Damn it. Don't make me do that."

Fargo gazed to the east, seeking sign of their quarry. Given how slow Mabel and her calf traveled, he figured the Hollisters couldn't be more than another mile or two ahead.

"You're not what I expected," Crown unexpectedly said.

"Why expect anything?"

"Someone half famous like you, folks love to gossip. I've heard their stories. About how you are lightning with a pistol, and hard as nails."

"I like my lightning in a bottle."

"They say that about you, too. You drink, you whore, you play a lot of cards."

"I listen to idiots talk about me."

Crown laughed again, and groaned again. "Damn it. Stop doing that."

"Is there a point to this?"

The bounty hunter nodded. "The stories don't tell all of it."

"When do they ever?"

"See? That's what I mean. They say you're snake-mean and booze-blind half the time, but you're not. There's more to you."

"I keep it hid in my pants."

This time when Crown stopped laughing he didn't wheeze as much. "I take back what I said. You are snake-mean. I asked you to stop doing that."

"I will if you stop jabbering."

"All I'm trying to say," Rafer Crown said, "is that you'd do to ride the river with."

"Do we hug now?"

Crown exploded in mirth and more cussing. "Can't you ever be serious?"

"Are you up to more running?"

"For her I am."

Fargo didn't push quite as hard. It wouldn't do to have the bounty hunter collapse because he was too worried about Aramone to stop and rest.

The tracks were easy enough to follow. Between all their horses and Thunderhead and his little family, a ten-year-old couldn't lose them.

Thinking of the horses made Fargo think of the Ovaro, and how Kyler Hollister said he'd taken a shine to the stallion and might keep it for his own.

Over Fargo's dead body.

By the sun it wasn't much past one when Fargo came to where the Hollisters had stopped for a while to let the calf rest. A pile of bull droppings was so fresh, they squished when he poked them with a stick. "We're not far behind."

"I hope not. I can't run much farther without my legs giving out."

It wasn't half an hour later, as they were descending a ridge, that Fargo spied a line of riders lower down, and the enormous longhorn.

Crown spotted them, too. "Do you see her anywhere?"

"Third in line," Fargo said.

"They haven't harmed her yet, then. Thank God."

Fargo was relieved, himself.

"How do you want to do this? Jump them now or wait until they stop for the night."

"If we wait," Fargo said, "will I have to listen to you gripe all damn day about how worried you are over her?"

"You will."

"Then as someone said to me earlier, let's get to killing those Hollisters."

51

The calf was the problem. It could only go a short way before it had to stop. And often when it stopped, it nursed.

The Hollisters were heartless bastards but they knew that if they made it easy for the calf, they'd reach the ranch sooner. So they made it as easy as they could by sticking to open ground wherever possible.

Along about the middle of the afternoon they halted on a grass tableland and the calf nursed.

Fargo could hear Kyler complaining as he crawled toward them.

"—tried of that stinkin' critter slowin' us. For two bits I'd plug it."

"You do and I'll plug you," Rance said.

"That's a fine thing to say to your own brother."

"We kill the calf, it'll upset the cow," Rance said. "We upset the cow, it'll upset the bull. We upset the bull, he might take it into his head to gore us or go wandering off. And since there's no way to stop him short of killin' him, we'd be out the five thousand dollars."

"This sure is gettin' complicated," Grizz said.

"We leave the calf be and it will be easy."

Kyler gestured at the bovines. "You call this easy? It's work, is what it is, herdin' these three. And I hate work more than I hate just about anything."

"Think of your share of the bounty," Rance said. "That should smooth your feathers."

"I ain't stupid," Kyler said. "I wouldn't really shoot the damned nuisance."

"Then quit your gripin'."

By then Fargo was behind a boulder not twenty feet from them.

He was relieved to see the Ovaro over with the other horses. And he imagined that Rafer Crown was relieved to see Aramone, her wrists bound, gazing forlornly up the mountain.

Rance Hollister took notice of her, too. "Which one of them is it, woman?"

"I don't know what you're talking about," Aramone replied.

"Like hell you don't. You've been moonin' over one or the other all damn day."

"I bet it's that Fargo fella," Grizz said. "He has a beard like me."

"What the hell does hair have to do with it?" Kyler said. "No, she's partial to the bounty hunter. I saw the look she gave him as we were ridin' off. About made me puke."

"By now the Blackfeet will have done them in," Rance remarked.

"You don't know that," Aramone said resentfully.

Rance's brow knit. "You know, she's right. We don't. One of us should ride back and have a look-see."

"What the hell for?" Kyler said. "Even if she is, they're still tied to those trees."

"They might have got free," Rance said.

"So? We're too far ahead for them to ever catch us."

"As slow as we're movin'," Rance said, "I'm not so sure."

"I'll go have that look if you want," Grizz offered.

Fargo got his hopes up that one or the other would ride off, but Rance shook his head.

"No. I've changed my mind. The three of us are more than a match for them or anyone else."

"You have that right, big brother," Kyler said. "We're hellions born and bred."

"I never knew jackasses brayed so much," Aramone said.

All three turned and Kyler stepped over and jabbed a finger in her face.

"Keep it up. You've mouthed off at us all day and I've had my fill. We might need to keep that calf alive but the same doesn't go for you."

"I have an idea," Grizz said.

Rance and Kyler looked at him as if they couldn't believe their ears. Rance even said, "You?"

"We take turns pokin' her and then I strangle her and we don't have to listen to her anymore."

"For you that's a brainstorm," Kyler said.

Grizz smiled and nodded. "I have one now and then."

"Every ten years," Kyler said.

"We save her for tonight," Rance said. "I'm partial to havin' my pokes right before I turn in."

"Well, hell," Kyler said. "A poke is a poke."

"I sleep better after I have one."

Now it was Kyler and Grizz who stared at their brother as if he were peculiar.

"Not me," Grizz said. "Whores usually snore and keep me awake."

"Is that why you damned near smothered that one in Denver?" Kyler asked.

"No. She was pickin' her nose and wipin' her finger on the sheets. I can't stand snot so I made her stop."

"You are a wonderment," Rance said.

"I have an idea," Aramone broke in. "How about if I ride back to see if they're still tied to those trees?"

"Funny gal," Rance said.

"Do we look stupid to you?" Kyler barked.

"Do I really need to answer that?"

Coloring red with anger, Kyler went to say something but froze, his gaze drifting past her toward the horses.

Rance looked, too.

So did Fargo, and was dumbfounded. He'd told Crown not to make a move until he did, but the bounty hunter had thrown caution to the winds and was making a try for the saddlebags with their weapons in them.

Crown had crawled as close as he could without being seen and risen into a crouch to run the last ten feet or so.

Snapping his Sharps to his shoulder, Rance Hollister said, "Try and you die."

52

Fargo hoped the bounty hunter would have the sense to throw his hands up and not move. But then Crown glanced at Aramone, and common sense went out the window with the dishwater.

Breaking into motion, Crown dashed to the horse. The Sharps boomed but Rance only knocked off Crown's hat. Kyler started toward him, brandishing his long knife, while Grizz clawed for the six-shooter wedged under his belt.

Fargo was nearest to Grizz. He heaved up and hurtled at him with his shoulder low.

Grizz must have caught sight of him because he tried to turn and point his pistol.

Fargo slammed into the slab of dumb low in the back. It was like slamming into a wall. He recovered and delivered an uppercut that, by rights, should have felled Grizz where he stood. Instead, Grizz dropped the revolver and wrapped his huge hands around Fargo's throat.

Fargo was vaguely aware of Aramone yelling and of Rance hollering to Grizz about getting out of the way so he had a clear shot. He glimpsed Crown and Kyler grappling and Kyler trying to bury his knife, and then his vision blurred and he couldn't breathe.

"I've got you now, mister," Grizz gloated.

Not if Fargo could help it. He drove his right knee into Grizz's crotch. Once, twice, and Grizz gurgled and his thick fingers loosened. Fargo rammed his other knee up and in, and Grizz squeaked like a mouse and tottered, cupping himself.

Fargo punched Grizz in the throat. Looking panicked, Grizz thrust out a hand and backpedaled. Fargo went after him, blocking a left and hitting Grizz in the throat a second time. He didn't hold back.

Grizz's eyes bulged and his mouth worked but only mews of pain and bewilderment came out. He swallowed, or tried to, and sucked in air through his nose.

Fargo waded in again. Grizz brought up both fists but he was swaying and his eyelids were drooping. Fargo struck him in the throat yet again.

Something crunched, and blood spurted from Grizz's mouth. Tottering, he grasped his neck. His tree-trunk legs buckled and he oozed to the grass.

Fargo whirled to help Crown. The bounty hunter and Kyler were on the ground, grappling and rolling.

Rance had run over and was attempting to fix a bead with the Sharps.

Aramone appeared transfixed with horror.

That was when a rifle cracked. But it wasn't the Sharps.

Rance Hollister tilted back, a hole high on his forehead. He looked as surprised as Fargo.

Kyler, who was on top of Crown, glanced up—and his left eye dissolved to another blast.

"What in the world?" Aramone blurted.

Fargo turned toward the woods as three figures emerged with their rifles leveled.

Rafer Crown shoved Kyler off and saw them, too. "What in hell? What are *they* doing here?"

The redheaded Johnson boys were grinning in delight. Solomon was in the middle, Seth to his right, Jared to his left.

"What do you think we're doin', mister?" Seth said, and laughed.

"Surprised to see us?" Solomon said to Fargo.

"Not as surprised as that farmer and the old woman must have been," Fargo said.

"He's figured it out, brothers," Seth said.

"I believe he has," Solomon said.

"Do we kill them now?" Jared asked.

"Kill us?" Aramone said in confusion. "Why, you're just children. You can't kill people."

Solomon laughed. "We just killed that jasper with the Sharps and the other one with the knife, didn't we?"

"We've killed a heap of folks," Seth bragged.

"We like it," little Jared said.

Aramone looked at Fargo. "Am I losing my mind? Am I imagining this?"

"They aim to claim the bounty no matter what they have to do," Fargo said.

Solomon nodded. "Five thousand is more than most folks earn in all their born days."

"We'll go on a spree," Seth said. "Me, I aim to eat so much hard candy, my gut will hurt."

"I want chocolate," Jared said.

"You can't be serious, boys," Aramone said. "This is insane."

Unnoticed by everyone save Fargo, the gunshots and commotion had angered Thunderhead. He stood in front of Mabel and the calf, his great head lowered, his front legs splayed, ready to slay anyone who came close.

"Lady, every time you open your mouth," Solomon was saying, "you say something dumb."

"How many of the bull hunters have you killed?" Rafer Crown asked.

"What's it to you?" Seth shot back.

"Nine," Solomon said, "besides that plow-pusher and the old bitch."

"Dear God," Aramone said.

"I am sick of all this gab," Jared told his freckled siblings. "Can we kill them and get this over with?"

Solomon looked at Fargo. "What do you think, mister? Should we? Or do you want to go on breathin' for a minute or two yet?"

"Kids, by God," Rafer Crown said. "I refuse to have it be you three."

"You don't have a choice, mister," Solomon said.

"Like hell I don't." Rafer spun and lunged at his horse but he'd barely moved his legs when Seth's squirrel rifle blasted. Rafer stumbled and clutched the bay's saddle to keep from falling.

Aramone cried, "You shot him!"

"We sure did," Solomon said, taking aim at the bounty hunter. "And now I'll finish him off."

Fargo was about to rush the redheaded terrors to try to stop them when there was a tremendous bellow.

Thunderhead had had enough. The gunshots, the yells, the screams, had frayed his temper to the snapping point.

Horns low, he hurtled at the Johnsons.

There was nothing Fargo could do. Why the longhorn picked them and not him or Aramone or Crown, he'd never know. Maybe it was their red hair. Bulls hated the color red, or so everyone said.

Whatever the case, Thunderhead was on them in a fury. Jared fired but the shot had no effect. It was like a ten-ton boulder slamming into three twigs. Thunderhead butted Solomon, crushing his chest, and slashed his long horns right and left.

Just like that, it was over.

Aramone let out a wail.

Fargo braced for the bull to whirl and attack them.

But no. Thunderhead turned and went to Mabel and the calf. His anger had evaporated as quickly as it exploded. Touching his muzzle to hers, he appeared perfectly peaceful.

Rafer Crown was on his feet, but wobbly. Aramone ran to him and looped both her arms around his waist.

"You're bleeding."

"That's usually what happens when someone is shot."

Not taking his eyes off the longhorns, Fargo sidled to the Ovaro, yanked his Henry from the scabbard, and only then asked, "How bad?"

"The kid clipped my shoulder," Crown said. "I'll live."

"You'd better," Aramone said, and kissed him on the cheek.

Crown stared at all the crumpled forms and once again gave voice to Fargo's own opinion. "This has been some mess."

"It's over, thank God," Aramone said. "I'll bandage you and you can rest."

"Rest, hell," Crown said. "We're taking that bull to the Bar T and collecting the bounty."

"Fine by me," Fargo said. He had some serious drinking to do. And then there was Candice, who wanted to show how grateful she was. By now she would have healed enough that she could.

Fargo smiled. Things were looking up.

LOOKING FORWARD!
**The following is the opening
section of the next novel in the exciting
Trailsman series from Signet:**

**TRAILSMAN #386
NEVADA VIPERS' NEST**

*Carson Valley, Nevada Territory, 1861—where Skye Fargo must
track down an elusive, mysterious woman or
be branded a murderer of women and children.*

Skye Fargo's stallion always showed a distinctive quiver in his
nostrils when he whiffed death.

And they had begun that quivering now as Fargo started to
ascend a low ridge overlooking the remote Carson Valley at the
western edge of the newly formed Nevada Territory.

Fargo expelled a weary, fluming sigh as he reined in. "Steady
on, old campaigner," he told his nervous Ovaro. "You know that
trouble never leaves us alone for very long."

The buckskin-clad man some called the Trailsman sat tall in
the saddle, his alert, lake-blue eyes watching his surroundings
from a weather-bronzed, crop-bearded face. He was wide in the
shoulders, slim in the hips, and a dusty white hat left half his face
in shadow.

The deadly alkali flats of Nevada stretched out to infinity
behind him, the majestic, ascending folds of the California Sierra
rose before him. Fargo was currently employed by the army as an

express messenger between Camp Floyd, in the Utah Territory, and Fort Churchill in Nevada.

Normally his route would not take him this far west into the silver-mining country. But the Paiutes, Bannocks and Shoshones in this region—no tribes to fool with—had recently made common cause to war on whiteskins. Fargo had been forced to flee in this direction to shake a war party determined to lift his dander.

And now this new trouble . . .

"Caught between a sawmill and a shootout," Fargo muttered. "Story of my life."

He clucked at his nervous stallion and gigged him up to a trot, sliding his brass-framed Henry rifle from its boot. The ridge he now ascended was strewn with boulders, and Fargo's slitted eyes stayed in constant scanning motion, watching for dry-gulchers.

Near the top of the ridge he spotted buzzards wheeling in a cloudless sky of bottomless blue—merchants of death impatient to feast. But the fact that they were still circling told Fargo that someone, human or animal, was likely still alive below.

Just before he topped the long ridge, he detected motion in the corner of his left eye.

With the honed reflexes of a civet cat, Fargo threw the reins forward and rolled from the saddle, levering a round into the Henry's chamber even before he landed on the ground. He peered cautiously past the Ovaro's shoulder, eyes widening in surprised disbelief.

In this dreary and woman-scarce country, the woman he now clearly spotted fleeing between boulders stood out like a brass spittoon in a funeral parlor. Evidently Fargo had ridden too close and scared her out of hiding.

"Hey!" he called out. "No need to skedaddle, lady! Maybe I can help you."

She paused for a moment, turning in his direction. Fargo drank in the thick tresses of copper-colored hair, flawless mother-of-pearl skin, a pretty, fine-boned face. But her sprigged-muslin dress was obscenely splotched with blood.

"What happened?" Fargo called to her, stepping out into the open.

By way of reply, the woman brought her right hand into view and fired a short iron at Fargo. The bullet came nowhere near him, but the surprised Trailsman leaped back behind his stallion.

"Christ, lady, lower the hammer! I want to help you. Are you hurt?"

"No, and I'm not going to be!" she shouted back. "If you even try to get any closer to me, I'm going to use every bullet but one in this gun to try to kill you. And if I miss, I'll use the last bullet on myself! I swear to God I will!"

The sheer desperation in her voice told Fargo she had recently suffered some unspeakable horror. He believed she meant every word.

"All right, lady, it's your call. But listen to me. If you turn to your right you'll be headed due south. Carson City is only three miles from here in that direction. If you keep going east like you are now, you'll die in the desert."

She must have heard him because she did turn south, disappearing among a clutch of boulders.

Fargo turned the stirrup, took up the reins, and stepped up and over. A minute later he topped the ridge and saw the whole bloody chronicle, laid out below like a tableau straight from hell.

"Shit, oh, dear," he muttered, fighting to control his sidestepping stallion, who wanted nothing to do with the scene below.

A sudden squall of anger tightened Fargo's lips and facial muscles. Despite everything he had seen during his many years yondering on the western frontier, there were some things he had never learned to stomach.

Especially the brutal murder of women and children.

A burned-out prairie schooner, still sending up curls of smoke, lay on its side, six dead Cleveland Bays tangled in the traces, all shot through their heads. A man, a woman and two small girls lay scattered about like ninepins, bodies riddled with bullet holes. The woman's calico dress had been pulled up and her chemise and pantaloons ripped away—clearly she had been raped before she was murdered.

Fargo also saw why the buzzards were still wheeling instead of swooping in for the feast. A man stood beside a blaze-faced sorrel, his face ashen as he surveyed the grisly scene.

"Rider coming in!" Fargo called out, bringing his Henry down to the level.

The man scarcely seemed to hear or notice the new arrival, still staring around him in a state of shock.

"Mister, you're either an innocent passerby or one damn fine actor," Fargo greeted him as he dismounted.

The man said nothing to this, his unblinking eyes like two glazed marbles. Fargo gave him a quick size-up. He was of medium height and build with a homely, careworn face and an unruly shock of dark hair. With his usual abundance of caution, Fargo kept the Henry leveled on him, but he strongly doubted that the stranger had played a hand in this slaughter.

Fargo glanced at the unusual firearm tucked behind the man's canvas belt.

"I see you play the harmonica," Fargo said, meaning the harmonica pistol the man carried. "Mind if I take a look at it?"

Fargo knew damn well that a small-caliber pistol didn't do the killing here. The dead man's heart had practically been ripped out of his body by a large-bore weapon. But the Trailsman hadn't survived so long by coming to quick conclusions.

"Snap out of your shit!" Fargo barked when the man failed to respond. "I said let me glom that harmonica."

Fargo's take-charge voice did rouse the man from his stupor. He handed the weapon over. It was an early attempt at a multishot pistol. A sliding bar held ten bullets with primer caps, the mechanism roughly resembling a harmonica. Each time the weapon was fired, the bar could be slid to the next round. The harmonica pistol had never caught on, though, because it was awkward and cumbersome.

"All right, mister," Fargo said, handing the weapon back. "Give."

"Not much to give," he replied. "I just got here about ten minutes before you did. I didn't see or hear anything."

"What brings you to these parts?"

"You might say I had to take the geographic cure, and in a puffin' hurry. I was working as a trick-whip performer for Doctor Geary's traveling medicine show. We were up north in Virginia City on the Comstock. I got into a poker game, and somehow a fifth ace turned up."

"Musta been a faulty deck," Fargo said sarcastically. "Where you headed?"

"Just drifting through to Old Sac," he replied, meaning Sacramento.

"What's your name?"

"Mitt McDougall, but I prefer to be called Sitch."

"Sitch . . . that's an unusual handle," Fargo remarked absently, beginning to study the ground around them for sign.

"It's bobtail for troublesome 'situations,' which I always find myself in—just like this one. Katy Christ, mister, did Indians do this?"

"Not unless they've taken to riding iron-shod horses and rolling cigarettes. There's several fresh butts here."

"And they call the red men savages. If it was road agents or whatever, why in Sam Hill did they have to slaughter all these folks just to rob them?"

"That don't cipher," Fargo agreed. "I've never heard of road agents deliberately killing women and children. Even the hardest of the hard twists shy away from that. Well, we best try to find out who these folks were before we bury them."

So far Fargo had avoided looking at the victims, but now he steeled himself for what must be done. He grounded his Henry, knelt beside the dead man, and started searching through his pockets.

Suddenly, the Ovaro gave his trouble whicker.

Fargo started to reach for his rifle when a shot split the silence, a geyser of sand spuming up only inches from his feet.

"Both you murdering sons a bitches freeze!" shouted a gravelly voice that brooked no defiance. "Make one damn move and we'll shoot you to rag tatters!"

THE LAST OUTLAWS
The Lives and Legends of Butch Cassidy and the Sundance Kid

by Thom Hatch

Butch Cassidy and the Sundance Kid are two of the most celebrated figures of American lore. As leaders of the Wild Bunch, also known as the Hole-in-the-Wall Gang, they planned and executed the most daring bank and train robberies of the day, with an uprecedented professionalism.

The Last Outlaws brilliantly brings to life these thrilling, larger-than-life personalities like never before, placing the legend of Butch and Sundance in the context of a changing—and shrinking—American West, as the rise of 20th century technology brought an end to a remarkable era. Drawing on a wealth of fresh research, Thom Hatch pushes aside the myth and offers up a compelling, fresh look at these icons of the Wild West.

**Available wherever books are sold or at
penguin.com**